"When did you get married?" Silas asked carelessly.

He had started to move off in the direction of the house, and Kate had automatically followed him. Now she stopped, almost missing her step.

"I'm not married," she told him indistinctly as he swung around to stare, frowning, at her. "I never have been married," she elucidated proudly, her chin tilting, her eyes defying him to comment.

There was a brief hiatus, and then he asked evenly, "And the man who fathered your child, are you and he still together? Did you dump him, too?"

His words were bitterly unfair, and angry tears burned at the back of her eyes. He had no idea at all that Cherry was his child....

PENNY JORDAN was constantly in trouble in school because of her inability to stop daydreaming—especially during French lessons. In her teens she was an avid romance reader, although it didn't occur to her to try writing one herself until she was older. "My first half-dozen attempts ended up ingloriously," she remembers, "but I persevered, and one manuscript was finished." She plucked up the courage to send it to a publisher, convinced her book would be rejected. It wasn't, and the rest is history! Penny is married and lives in Cheshire.

Books by Penny Jordan

Don't miss any of our special offers. Write to us at the following address for information on our newest releases.

Harlequin Reader Service
901 Fuhrmann Blvd., P.O. Box 1397, Buffalo, NY 14240
Canadian address: P.O. Box 603,
Fort Erie, Ont. L2A 5X3

PENNY JORDAN

potential danger

Harlequin Books

TORONTO • NEW YORK • LONDON
AMSTERDAM • PARIS • SYDNEY • HAMBURG
STOCKHOLM • ATHENS • TOKYO • MILAN

Harlequin Presents first edition August 1989
ISBN 0-373-11193-2

Original hardcover edition published in 1988
by Mills & Boon Limited

CHAPTER ONE

'HOW much longer, Mum?'

Kate Seton looked down into her daughter's face, alive with the excitement and impatience of a ten-year old, on the threshold of a much promised treat, and wishing the miles of their journey away because of it.

Once, she too had been impatient of this long journey from London to the Yorkshire Dales, but her anxious need had been to travel away from the Dales, not to them, and she had been eighteen and not ten.

That she had also been pregnant and terrified was something she preferred not to think about today. The journey home was not just a treat for Cherry; it was also something of a fence-mending exercise with her own parents. She sighed faintly and closed her eyes, blotting out the familiar landscape of summer greens.

They had travelled through the once great industrial heartland of the country and had emerged into the tranquil greenery of a land that bore its scars of age and hardship proudly.

Like its people. Like her parents.

'Mum, will my grandfather really be there to meet us?'

All the anxiety of a child who had learned not to expect too much from the adult world was in

Cherry's voice, and it hurt Kate to hear that uncertainty.

'Yes, he will,' she assured her.

And he would. If her father said he would do something, do it he would. It was a trait inherent among the farming community of the Dales, bred into them by their environment and necessity.

She watched Cherry while her daughter stared excitedly out of the window. She had named her Cherry because she had been born in the month of May when the cherry trees were in blossom. It had been for Cherry's sake that she had left the Dales, and it was now, ironically, for her sake that she was returning.

'And we really will be staying with Granny and Grandpa for all the summer holidays, won't we?' Cherry asked her anxiously, diverted from the study of the unfamiliar scenery to question her mother.

'Yes,' Kate answered her calmly, but inside she was far from feeling calm. How would her parents react to this grandchild they had never seen?

Eighteen, unmarried and pregnant, she had left home in disgrace after announcing her pregnancy to her parents.

Her father had a very strict, unbending moral code; it had driven David, Kate's elder brother, to leave home at seventeen and to roam the world before finally settling down in Canada. She had been twelve at the time that David had left, and her father had seen his son's departure as a desertion of his duty to follow him on the farm.

Setons had farmed in Abbeydale since the days

of the Reformation, clinging to their upland pastures with the same tenacity as the sheep they bred, and to John Seton it was unthinkable that his only son should want to break away from a tradition that had endured for many hundreds of years.

With the hindsight of adult perception, Kate could see how her father's crippling disappointment in David's desertion had tainted his life and coloured his attitude towards her.

He had been a strict father, but not oppressively so; after school she had been expected to help out around the farm, sharing her mother's chores of raising chickens and selling eggs, cultivating the kitchen garden in the walled lea of the house where they grew fresh fruit and vegetables, but she had hated the restrictiveness of her existence.

Perhaps that was why she had worked so hard at school, knowing that the opportunity to go to university would be her only means of escape.

If there was one thing her father respected, it was education, and so when the time came, albeit reluctantly, he had driven Kate down to the station to see her off on the journey that would take her away from the farm for ever.

How lonely and terrified she had been those first few weeks at Lancaster University; how very different the reality from her imaginings. The other girls were so much more sophisticated than her; she felt excluded and alone.

And then she had met Silas.

'Mum, did my father come from the Dales?'

Her head snapped round, the dark green eyes

she had inherited from a Scottish ancestress wide and vulnerable.

By what uncanny mental telepathy had Cherry picked up on her thoughts and asked her that question?

Cherry rarely mentioned her father. She knew that she was the result of a brief liaison her parents had shared while at university, and she accepted the fact that her father had no place in her life, nor wanted one, without any apparent concern. So many of the children she was at school with were in the same position that it was barely worthy of comment.

How different things had been ten years ago when Cherry was born. How *her* father had ranted and railed against the shame an illegitimate grandchild would bring to their name. Such things didn't happen to Setons . . . To be sure, there had been the odd rushed marriage in the family's history, the odd seven-months child; but in those days modern mores had not yet reached the Dales, and there had been no way Kate could have stayed at home and kept her child.

And so she had taken the only option open to her. She had walked from the farm to the local station, half blinded by her own tears; terrified beyond belief by what she was doing, but urged on by the inherent stubbornness that was part of the Seton heritage. She was not going to give up her child.

She realised with a start that she hadn't answered Cherry's question and that her daughter was regarding her curiously.

'No . . . no . . . he didn't,' she told her truthfully, and then added in warning, 'Don't mention him to your grandparents, Cherry, will you?'

'Did they know him?' Cherry asked her, obviously puzzled by her instruction.

Kate shook her head. 'No.'

And it was true. Her parents had never met Silas. She had been planning to take him home with her at Christmas. They had been going to announce their engagement, or so she had believed. God, she had been a fool . . . But what was the point in thinking about that now? She had been a fool as so many naïve girls were fools and would go on being fools. It was impossible to change human emotions, and girls would continue to fall in love and give themselves in the intensity of that love, to men who were simply using them to satisfy the immediacy of their sexual urges.

She reached out and pushed her daughter's thick, dark hair back off her face. Cherry's hair was a legacy from Silas. It had that same raven's wing sheen, and her eyebrows his expressive lift.

She had the green Seton eyes, though, set in a face whose delicate heart shape promised to mirror her own, once the softening influence of childhood disappeared.

Her own hair was a dark, rich red and thickly curly. It vibrated with its own electric intensity, and Silas had often teased her that she was so small and tiny because all her strength went into her hair.

That was one way in which she and Cherry

were not alike. Cherry promised to be tall like her
father. One day, her daughter was going to be an
extremely beautiful woman, Kate reflected, and it
was Silas's loss that he would not be able to witness the wonder of that woman emerging. Kate
was determined that her daughter would be a
woman of the eighties—feminine, warm, intelligent, honest, self-reliant—and she wondered
briefly and treacherously how she would
compare to Silas's other children: those two dark-
haired boys whose existence she had never even
guessed at in the days when she had been drunk
on love and pleasure, and believing that Silas
belonged to her alone.

Heady days; days which would have been little
more than a memory, perhaps, if it hadn't been
for Cherry.

It seemed odd now to remember that she had
ever been such a creature of passion and intensity
that she had conceived a child.

Those fires had long ago burned out, smother-
ed by layer upon layer of panic, pain, confusion,
and the sheer hard work of building a life for
herself and her child.

'I wish Aunt Lydia could have come with us,
don't you?'

Aunt Lydia was in fact Kate's godmother; the
true fairy-story kind of godmother, who had
taken her in as a homeless, terrified eighteen-
year-old, stood by her through Cherry's birth,
supported, advised and, most important of all,
loved them both. And now, finally she had been
the active force in breaking down the barriers of

the eleven-year-old silence between Kate and her parents.

Knowing quite well that Cherry's comment sprang from a sudden surge of nervousness at meeting the grandparents she had never known, Kate responded carelessly, 'Aunt Lydia hates the countryside, love, you know that. Can you honestly see her in wellies and muddy fields?' she asked mischievously.

Lydia was a town creature, all brittle, elegant bones and long, polished nails, her outward appearance belying her kind nature.

How she and her mother had ever become friends in the first place, never mind kept that friendship alive for over thirty years, was a mystery to Kate, but somehow they had.

They were really in the Dales now, travelling through long upland valleys, green with pastures, and the odd stand of trees, dotted with small, clinging, stone farmhouses.

Cherry was fascinated, almost glued to the carriage window.

Kate had lost count of the number of times her daughter had asked her about Abbeydale and her grandparents since that Christmas telephone call.

Initially, she herself hadn't wanted to come; she was frightened that doing so would arouse too many painful memories. But Lydia had reminded her gently that there were others whose feelings must be considered, Cherry in particular.

'She's a Seton, Kate,' she had pointed out quietly. 'She loves the countryside. Times have changed. Illegitimacy isn't the slur it was. Your father was wrong in behaving as he did, but he and your mother both miss and love you.'

'Cherry wants to be a vet,' Kate had responded illogically, and she had seen Lydia smile, that secret, pleased smile that showed she knew she had won a victory. And so here they were, within minutes now of the meeting she had been secretly fearing ever since it had been arranged.

The train slowed down, crawled through a tunnel and emerged into the golden sunlight of the July afternoon.

The small station was bedecked with hanging baskets and flowering plants, its name picked out proudly in fresh paint, but, as Kate got up to collect her things and usher Cherry towards the door, she saw no sign of her father on the platform.

Then, if she could have done so, she would have turned round and gone right back to London. That was where she belonged now. That was where her life lay, teaching as she had done ever since she had qualified.

She enjoyed her work; it held a multiplicity of challenges that constantly re-energised her; she loved the children themselves and she loved teaching them.

The train stopped. She paused before opening the door. No one else got out, and she had a sensation of stepping back in time, of being eighteen again and newly home from university.

And surely that was Mr Meadows waiting to take their tickets?

He had seemed ancient to her at eighteen, but he

was probably only in his sixties now, Kate recognised as she handed over the slips of paper with a smile.

'Your dad's waiting for you in the car park,' he told her, eyeing her with friendly recognition. 'And this is the young 'un, is it? Spit of your ma, isn't she?'

'Am I like Grandma?' Cherry asked her curiously as they walked through the booking hall.

'A little . . .'

Only in that she was like herself, Kate suspected. Her parents were second cousins, Setons both; both spare and wiry, and in some ways very physically alike. Her mother's hair had never been as red as Kate's, and it had certainly been nothing like Cherry's polished waterfall of straight ebony.

There was only one vehicle in the car park, an ancient Land Rover, with a man standing beside it.

Kate felt the apprehension curl through her stomach. In addition to rearing and breeding sheep, her father trained prize sheep-dogs, and throughout her childhood there had never been one of these animals far from his side. There was one at his feet now, a quiver of intelligent black and white fur, the sight of which transfixed Cherry to the spot in delighted disbelief.

While her daughter studied the dog, Kate studied her father. He had aged—but then, hadn't they all?—and working in a climate like the Dales, twelve hours a day, seven days a week,

took its toll on the human frame, even one as
hardy as her father's.

He returned her look a little defensively, and
then, ridiculously, she felt tears prick her eyes
and she did something she had never intended to
do, practically running across the car park to hug
him.

He returned her embrace awkwardly, uncertainly, like a man unused to demonstrations of
physical caring, and then released her to say
gruffly, 'Aye, she's a proper Seton,' and Kate
could have sworn there was just a suspicion of
moisture in his eyes as he looked at her daughter.

'The man at the station said I was the image of
my grandma,' Cherry told him importantly.

Instantly he scowled. 'That Tom Meadows
always had a fancy for your mother,' he told Kate
irefully.

'Grandpa, is it all right for me to stroke your
dog?' Cherry asked him formally.

Again he scowled, and Kate, well acquainted
with her father's view that dogs were working
animals and best treated as such, was astounded
to see him suddenly bend and fondle the silky
black and white coat with gentle fingers. His
hand was gnarled. An old man's hand, she
recognised shockingly.

'Aye, I don't see why not. His name's Laddie.'

Lassie, Laddie, Meg, Skip—those were always
the names her father chose for his dogs. A dog
trained by John Seton was always in high
demand, but for as long as she could remember
Kate had never known her father sell a dog to a

man he didn't like.

As Cherry bent down to stroke the dog, crooning happily as his tail beat on the dusty ground, Kate asked, 'Will you be working him in the county show, Dad?'

'No, not this one. He's not much good as a worker.'

He saw the astonishment on her face and added gruffly, 'Your mother took to him, though, and I couldn't get rid of him. Sleeps in the house an' all, he does.' He scowled horribly. 'Ought to have had him put down. Dog's no good if it can't work . . .'

Had she not seen with her own eyes the love in her father's face as he stroked his pet, Kate might almost have believed him.

How many times in the past had she been too ignorant or too immature to see that his gruff manner hid real emotion? She had thought him a cold, hard, man, and so she had run away from him and from her home, convinced that if she stayed he would make her hand over her baby for adoption.

And yet now, as he looked at Cherry, there was pride as well as grief in his eyes; love as well as regret.

'We'd better get on, then. No use standing about here giving folks cause to gossip. Besides, your ma will be waiting.'

The village hadn't changed at all. There was still the same bench outside the post office's wistaria-draped front wall, a meeting-point for the older members of the village. During the day it was normally occupied by the women, but in the evening it was the preserve of the men. Opposite the post office was the village's single pub, the De Burghley Arms. A rather grand name for a very small and homely building. It took its name from the follower of William the Conqueror who had once owned these lands; a family which had distant connections with Queen Elizabeth the First's famous minister.

The last de Burghley had left the village just before Kate, in the funeral cortège taking him to the family vault within the walls of their local parish church.

One of his ancestors, robed in the stone mimicry of his Crusader uniform, lay at rest within the church itself; and the church's stained-glass windows gave testimony to the many de Burghleys who, over the centuries, had given their lives in what they considered to be just causes.

It was her father's proud boast that there had been Setons in the dale for as long as there had been de Burghleys, if not longer. There was even a story in the family that the first Seton had been a wild raider from the Scottish borders who had tried to steal away one of the de Burghley daughters to hold for ransom, but who had ended up falling in love with her instead, and who had received from his new father-in-law, as the price of her dowry, the lands which the Setons had farmed ever since.

If that was the case, the dowry had not been an overgenerous one, Kate reflected as the engine note of the Land Rover changed and they started to climb the ribbon of grey road between its darker grey borders of dry stone walling.

Her family's acreage, though large, comprised not the rich pasture lands of the dale bottom, but the unproductive uplands fit only for sheep.

Once vast flocks of sheep had roamed the Seton lands, and in the Middle Ages the Setons had grown wealthy from their profit, but two World Wars and the death of her grandfather had reduced the flocks to a handful of worthless animals.

It had been her father who had had the foresight to see that the future lay in selective breeding, in producing not the world's wool, but the rams that would produce the flocks which would produce such wool.

Seton rams were famous and prized the world over, but, as Kate knew from her childhood, those early years of establishing their reputation had been hard ones for her parents, with long separations between them while her father travelled, mainly to South America, Australia and New Zealand, doing his own marketing. Her mother remained at home, in sole charge of the farm: her children, the livestock and her husband's precious ewes and lambs.

Through it all her parents had worked as a team, each selflessly working for the other. They had a relationship which now was considered old-fashioned, with her mother making her husband the pivot of her life.

The farm and their lives together here in the Dales; that had been the total sum of their ambitions. No wonder her father had been so disappointed when David had announced he wanted to be an engineer.

Kate had kept in sporadic touch with her brother and knew that he was married, but as yet had no children. Was that what had motivated her father to mend the breach between them? The fact that Cherry, her daughter, was the only member of the next generation?

Cherry was chattering to her grandfather as though she had known him all her life. Already there was a rapport between them completely unshadowed with the awe in which Kate herself had always held him.

Listening to Cherry talking knowledgeably to him about the sheep—throwing out snippets of facts she could only have picked up from her, Kate recognised—she was both amused and saddened by her daughter's grave, slightly old fashioned air. Cherry was such a contained, adult child in many ways, and yet in others she was so heartbreakingly vulnerable. This visit meant so much to her; she had talked of nothing else for months, ever since Lydia had dropped her bombshell at Christmas, by announcing that she had been in touch with Kate's mother and that her parents wanted her to go home, if only for a visit.

Kate ached to remind Cherry that a visit was all it could be, but was reluctant to cloud her daughter's happiness.

Cherry was a country child and bloomed in a country environment. She herself had ambivalent feelings towards the Dales. She loved them; they were her heritage and no one of any sensitivity, having known them, could cut that knowledge from her soul without destroying it.

But London had been good to her as well. London had provided her with a job, with independence, with a home for Cherry, where no one expressed surprise or curiosity over her lack of a father.

With Cherry herself she had been totally honest, explaining that she had fallen in love with her father, and that, having done so, she had only discovered too late that he was married to someone else.

What she had not told Cherry was that Silas and his wife had two children. She had not wanted to burden her daughter with that knowledge. It was enough that *she* carried it.

Thank God that was something her parents had never known, especially her father. They had simply believed that she had 'got herself into trouble' with someone at university, and that that someone, once he had realised she was pregnant, had turned his back on her. And she had let them think that it was as simple as that.

They were crossing what was de Burghley land now; the great house hidden from them by the trees planted all around it. As they passed the gates, Kate noticed a large notice-board attached to the wall, and the uniformed security guard standing outside the lodge house.

'What's happened to the Hall?' she questioned her father curiously.

De Burghley land ran alongside theirs, which no

doubt had given rise to that old story about a Seton having married a de Burghley daughter.

'Government's bought it,' her father told her abruptly. 'Started up some kind of monitoring unit there, where they do all kinds of special tests. All very hush-hush it is, and no one allowed inside the grounds, or on to the land for that matter, without permission. Opened up about twelve months ago. The man who runs it is a reasonable sort. Keeps himself to himself, but there's some locally say that it can only cause trouble . . .'

'What kind of trouble, Grandpa?' Cherry asked curiously.

Kate saw her father frown.

'The sort I don't know much about, lass,' he told her heavily, adding for Kate's benefit, 'Been a lot of ewes aborting this last year, and then all that business from Russia.'

Having correctly interpreted his remarks as a reference to the Chernobyl disaster which Kate knew from newspaper reports had badly affected lamb and cattle sales for meat, it was Kate's turn to frown.

She knew, of course, about the nuclear fall-out which had been rumoured to have affected some parts of the area, and of course no one could live in these times and not be aware of the fears caused by such places as Windscale, but to see the concern in her father's eyes brought the reality of it home to her.

'You're not saying that you've been affected by nuclear fall-out up here, Dad, are you?' she questioned him, immediately worried for Cherry, for who knew what effects even minute amounts of radiation could have on growing children?

'We're not told. But why else open this research station . . . and why keep it all so secret? There's a lot of concern in the village about it, I can tell you. Protest meetings and the like.'

'And the man who's in charge of the place—what does he say?'

'Says there's nothing to worry about, and I, for one, believe him.'

Because he wanted to believe him, Kate recognised. It would break her father's heart if anything happened to contaminate Seton land. She heard the pride in his voice as they rounded a turn in the road and passed the boundary that divided the de Burghley acres from their own.

'Now, lass,' he told Cherry, 'you're on Seton land. What dost tha think o' un?'

Cherry looked as though she were about to burst with pride and delight, and before Kate could stop her, and regardless of the fact that her father was driving the Land Rover, Cherry flung her arms round his neck and said ecstatically, 'Oh, Grandpa, I'm so glad that we're here.'

'Now . . . now enough of that . . .'

But her father was careful not to hurt her as he disengaged himself, Kate noticed, and she also noticed the surreptitious way in which he blew his nose only seconds later.

They entered the family farmyard to a cacophany of barking from the dogs, mingling with the cackle of her mother's hens and the bleating of half a dozen or so huge fat lambs, plainly those which had been hand-reared during the spring and which were now proving reluctant to return to the flock, Kate reflected, recognising the familiar pattern of her childhood.

'Watch out for the bantam,' her father warned them as he stopped the Land Rover.

'What's a bantam?' Cherry demanded.

'A small hen,' Kate told her, ruefully remembering her mother's affection for her bantam silkies and the ferocity of the minute males who lorded it over their harems.

'Don't tell me that Ma still keeps geese,' Kate groaned as she heard the familiar alarm sound. In her childhood, even her father had not been safe from the sharp beaks of her mother's geese, always excellent watchdogs. Their main fault was that it was impossible to teach them to discern between friend and foe.

And then the back door was opening and her mother was standing there. Not really changed at all. Her hair still neat and braided, her diminutive, wiry form still clad in a neat skirt and blouse, covered by an old-fashioned apron.

Across the yard Kate saw the look her parents exchanged, and she was at once a part and yet not a part of a magic circle that concentrated its love on the girl standing uncertainly on one foot as she stared round the unfamiliar yard.

'I've brought them then, Jean, love . . .'

And suddenly her mother's arms were open and both she and Cherry were caught up in them. Odd how so much strength could come from such a slight form. As she released them, Kate heard her mother saying tearfully, 'My, but she's the spitting image of you, John. A real Seton.'

And for the second time that day she was aware, as she had never been aware as a child, of the great love between her parents; for Cherry certainly looked like neither of them, since her features were hers, Kate knew, and her colouring and build was completely her father's.

But there was no time to reflect any more on Cherry's physical heritage, because she was crossing the familiar threshold into the the large square kitchen of her childhood, and the years were rolling back. She almost felt she could be Cherry's age again, just home from school, waiting for David to finish his chores so that they could sit down and eat.

'It's grand to have you home, lass.'

Quiet words, but full of emotion. Kate looked at her mother.

'It's lovely to be here, Mum. I don't think Cherry has talked of anything else since Christmas.'

'Cherry . . . what kind of name is that to give the child?' her father snorted.

And it was Cherry herself who answered him saying brightly, 'But Mum called me that because the cherry trees were in blossom when I was born.'

They had tea in the large, panelled dining-room that overlooked the gardens at the front of the house. Originally built as a minor hall, the house was much larger than the other stone farmhouses that populated the dale. It had a sunny drawing-

room that overlooked the dale itself and, although
the ground was barren and the winter winds icy,
in the protection of the walled garden countless
generations of Seton women had cultivated not
only fruit and vegetables, but flowers as well.

The drawing-room was only used on formal
occasions, its oak furniture lovingly waxed and its
parquet floor polished.

Normally they ate in the large kitchen; and in the
summer, as Kate remembered it, their evening
meal had often been as late as eight or nine in the
evening so that her father could make the most of
the long hours of daylight.

Tea was the word used to describe the evening
meal in the north, and not dinner, and on this
occasion her mother had baked all the things for
which she was justly famous in the dale: scones
light as feathers from her bantam chickens, bread,
still slightly warm from the old-fashioned bread
ovens either side of the new Aga and still used by
her mother, currant slices, lightly dusted with
sugar, summer pudding made from some of the
early fruits, the kind of salad that had never
dreamed of seeing the inside of a supermarket but
came straight from her mother's garden, and tiny
new potatoes, and home-cured ham. All the old-
fashioned things she remembered from her
childhood, and yet, as she sliced into her mother's
bread, Kate saw that it had been made with
wholemeal flour, showing that even up here
people were not totally immune to the power of
the Press.

Despite the excellence of the food, Kate wasn't

hungry. Cherry was, though, tucking into her food with the healthy appetite of the young.

Already Kate thought she could see a change in her—an opening up, a stretching out and growing—as though somehow she had been cramped in their city life.

Throughout the meal she chatted to her grandparents, telling them about her school and her friends, leaving Kate alone with her own thoughts.

It was disturbing how much Silas was occupying them. She supposed she ought to have expected it and been prepared for it, for, although Silas had never visited her home, the emotional trauma of her own leaving of it was bound to have left a lingering resonance for her sensitive nerves to pick up on.

And yet she had barely thought about him at all in years. He was part of her past, and for Cherry's sake she could not regret having known him, but the discovery that he had deceived her, that he was married with children, had totally killed her love.

And she had never allowed herself to fall into the same trap again.

Oh, she had dated—fellow schoolteachers, friends of friends who shared her interest in the theatre and with whom she had enjoyed pleasurable evenings—but there had been nothing like the intensity of emotion she had known with Silas.

Why not? She was emotionally and physically capable of that emotion, and yet, for some reason, after Silas she had had no other lovers, no man in her life who was more than a friend.

Was it perhaps because she had been afraid? Afraid of the vulnerability such a commitment would bring?

In the early years, of course, there had been Cherry. Most men shied away from a woman with a young child, and Kate's life had been too exhausting to allow her to do anything other than care for her child and complete her education. Without Lydia's help and love, even that much would not have been possible.

'I've put Cherry in your old room.'

Her mother's quiet words cut through her introspective thoughts.

Her old room. Tiny and cosy, up under the eaves, with its uneven walls and sloping ceiling.

'You're quite close to her . . . in the guest room. It's got its own bathroom now, and I thought you'd prefer that.'

A guest room with its own bathroom. Nostalgia touched her with melancholy fingers. Even here, after all, things changed. She had noticed that her parents had also had central heating installed. A new innovation, indeed. She remembered vividly the arguments when her mother had first tentatively broached the subject. Then her father had flatly refused to even consider it.

But times obviously changed. People changed.

CHAPTER TWO

LATER on that evening, as she took Cherry up to bed, sitting in the familiar bedroom with its rose-patterned wallpaper, Kate listened half-heartedly to her daughter's excited chatter, while part of her couldn't help remembering how she had thrown herself on this very bed and wept with grief and fear, unable to believe that she was actually pregnant . . . that Silas was actually married . . . that her father was refusing to allow her in the house.

'And Grandpa was saying that it will soon be the Dales Show. I wish I had something I could show. Mum, are you all right?'

Kate gave her a faint smile. 'Fine . . .'

'Were you thinking about my father?'

Green eyes met green, and Kate wondered at the perception of this child of hers, who could be so gravely and heart-breakingly mature.

And there was no doubt at all about where she got that perception from. It was one of the first things she had noticed about Silas . . . That and his almost overpoweringly male good looks.

She realised she was drifting helplessly back into the past and that she had not answered Cherry's question. Walking over to the window, she looked out at the familiar scenery of the dale. Below them, her father's sheep were gathered in the lowland pastures. These would be the ones that would soon need shearing.

Keeping her back toward Cherry, she said quietly, 'No. No, I wasn't thinking about your father. I was just remembering when this was my room.'

It was the first time she had lied to Cherry, and the small deception hurt, but coming home had stirred up too many memories, had brought to the surface of her consciousness feelings and thoughts she couldn't share with anyone.

Thoughts not just of Silas, but of David, her childhood, her parents and her own suddenly altered perceptions of past events; it was almost as though she had turned a corner and found herself confronted with an unfamiliar view of a territory so intimately well-known that the shock of the unexpected forced her to examine what she thought she had known.

'Time for bed,' she told Cherry, turning to smile at her. Whatever else she might think or feel, nothing could change her love for this child she and Silas had made together.

She kissed her, hugging her briefly.

'Happy to be here, Cherry?'

'Oh, yes . . . It's even better than I hoped.' She turned serious green eyes to her mother. 'If I lived here, I don't think I'd ever want to leave.' And the sombre look she gave the view from the window made Kate's heart tremble with apprehension.

The last thing she wanted was for Cherry to become too attached to this place. There was no way they could make their lives here on a permanent basis. Jobs in teaching in this part of the world were bound to be scarce, and where would they live, other than with her parents?

Seeing Cherry settled into bed, Kate went downstairs, automatically heading for the kitchen.

To her surprise only her father was there, engaged in the homely task of making a pot of tea. An unfamiliar sound caught her ears and she traced it to a dishwasher discreetly concealed by an oak panel that matched the rest of the kitchen.

'Your mother's not getting any younger,' her father said gruffly, noticing her astonishment. 'Time was when I hoped that David would change his mind and come back, but it looks like your mother and I will be the last Setons to live here, and I don't want your mother dying before her time through overwork.'

Kate could scarcely conceal her astonishment. What had happened to the stern, unyielding father who had never allowed either of his children to see any hint of what he might think of as weakness?

'Times change, lass,' he said heavily, as though he had seen into her mind. 'And sometimes they bring hard lessons. I was wrong to say to you what I did. Driving you out of your home like that . . . Hasty words spoken in the heat of the moment, and both of us too proud to back down, eh?'

Kate had never thought of it like that, never seen in her own refusal to risk rejection by getting in touch with her parents a mirror-image of her father's notorious pride, but now she saw that he was, in part, right.

'It took your mother to make me see sense, and

thank goodness she did. Yon's a fine lass you've got there. It will do your mother good to have someone to fuss over besides me and the shepherds.'

As he finished speaking Kate heard a whine outside the back door, and to her astonishment her father opened it to let in the dog who had accompanied him to the station.

'No good in the open, this one,' he told her slightly shamefacedly. 'I should have got rid of him, but I hadn't the heart. Spoiled him to death, your mother has.'

But Kate noticed, when her father carried the tea-tray through into the sitting-room, that it was at his feet that the dog lay.

With Cherry in bed, Kate felt oddly vulnerable and uncomfortable. She had left this house in fear and misery eleven years ago, and now she was back, but how could those years be bridged?

It proved to be astonishingly easy. It became apparent to Kate that there was scarcely a single feature of her and Cherry's lives that Lydia had left untold, and that her mother was almost as familiar with the regular pattern of their lives as she was herself.

Lydia had been a good friend to both of them, Kate recognised.

Quite what she had hoped to achieve by her precipitous flight to London she didn't really know, but after two terrifying days and nights of living rough she had suppressed her pride and gone to see her godmother.

Lydia had not, as she had dreaded, insisted on

Kate going home, or even agreed with her parents that her pregnancy must be hushed up and her child adopted. Instead she had offered Kate and her baby a home with her for just as long as they needed it.

A career woman with no ties, she had adapted remarkably well to the responsibility of a pregnant teenage girl, Kate thought. It had been Lydia who had encouraged her to go back to her studies and complete her degree, who had insisted on sharing the care of Cherry with her so that she was free to do so, and who had also encouraged her to buy her own small flat once she had finally got a job, thus giving both her and Cherry their independence.

Not once had she ever asked about Silas, and not once had Kate mentioned him. So why start thinking about him now? What was the point?

Her mother hadn't been wrong to remind her of her father's habit of early rising, Kate reflected ruefully the next morning when the sound of her father whistling to his dog woke her from her slumbers.

Without even going to the window, she could picture the scene in the yard below: her father in his ancient tweed jacket, crook in one hand, as he summoned his dog for the start of their day's work.

On a summer morning like this he would be working the fells, checking on his sheep and preparing his dogs for the Dales Show.

As she lay there, other sounds penetrated her

consciousness; the muted baaing of the wool-
sheep in the paddock on the far side of the
house; the cackling of her mother's hens and
then the impatient roar of her father's voice as he
called his dog to order.

They hadn't had a sheepdog yet unable to
resist the temptation of trying to round up the
hens, and Kate grinned to herself as she
burrowed deeper under the blankets. As a
teenager she had cherished every extra stolen
moment in bed in the mornings, but this
morning she couldn't recapture that teenage
pleasure. Instead she found she was thinking
about her mother, who would be busy
downstairs.

Groaning at the extra burdens of conscience
that adulthood brought, she started to get up,
pausing by her window and frowning as she
heard Cherry's excited voice floating up to her
from the yard.

'I'm up, Grandpa. Can I come with you?'

'You'll have to ask your mother about that,'
she heard her father growl. 'And you'll need
something inside you first.'

'But you will wait for me, won't you?' Cherry
persisted, and Kate found that she was holding
her breath, praying that her father wouldn't hurt
Cherry's feelings by refusing her request.

Half of her was already prepared for it when
he said brusquely, 'The fells are no place for
someone who doesn't know them,' but then, to
her surprise and relief, he softened his refusal by
adding more gently, 'You go in and speak to

your mother and have your breakfast, and then later on you can come and watch while I put Laddie through his paces in the paddock. Not that it will do the stupid creature the least bit of good. Never make a champion . . . Too soft, that's what he is.'

Kate was downstairs by the time Cherry came in, her small face alight with excitement.

'Mum, I'm going to help Gramps train Laddie,' she told Kate importantly.

And because she loved and understood her, Kate overlooked the small exaggeration and said instead, 'Are you, indeed? Well then, you're going to need something to eat first, aren't you?'

Cherry had always had a healthy appetite, but already the upland air seemed to have sharpened it, and Kate saw the pleasure touch her own mother's face as Cherry devoured the meal Jean had made for her.

'You should have let me do that, Mum,' Kate protested quietly, when Cherry had gone upstairs to clean her teeth. 'You've got enough to do already.'

'It's no trouble. It's a long time since I've had a young one to cook for,' she added quietly, and somehow her words underlined the loneliness of their lives, making Kate guiltily conscious that she could and should have done more earlier to heal the rift between them.

For too long she had retained her childhood perceptions of her parents and her father's anger, and now it hurt her to acknowledge that she might have been guilty of deliberately

holding on to her own anger and resentment.
They were both so patently thrilled with Cherry,
and she made up her mind there and then that
she would see to it that she made it up to both
Cherry and her parents for all the times together
they had missed.

When her father came back later in the
morning, Cherry rushed out to join him.

Watching her daughter skipping happily at her
grandfather's side with the black and white
collie, plumy tail waving happily from side to
side as it followed them, Kate felt an unexpected
prickle of tears sting her eyes.

She was standing in the kitchen at the
window, and behind her her mother said
quietly, 'I'm glad you came, love. Your dad's
missed you . . .'

'And David,' Kate acknowledged, blinking
away her tears. 'He was always his favourite.'

'No, you're wrong,' her mother insisted. 'If he
had a favourite, it was you. Some men are like
that. Real softies when it comes to their
daughters. Thinking the world of them, and
nothing too good for them. It was like that with
your dad. That's why . . .' She sighed and broke
off, but immediately Kate knew what she was
thinking. That was why her father had been so
shocked and so bitterly angry when she'd
announced her pregnancy.

How easy it was to understand his feelings
now, and how very, very difficult it had been at
the time.

'There's some letters to post. Why don't you

take the Land Rover and drive down to the village?' her mother suggested, and Kate wondered if she had sensed her sudden, aching need to be on her own to sort out the confusion of her own thoughts.

It had been a long time since she had driven a four-wheel-drive vehicle, but it was a skill that, once learned, was soon remembered, and by the time she had reached the village she was feeling confident enough to reverse the vehicle into a spot almost right opposite the small post office and general store.

Susan Edmonson, the postmistress, recognised her immediately, beaming a warm smile at her. Susan's dark hair was generously flecked with grey now and she was plumper than she had been, but she still possessed the same intense curiosity about her fellow human beings that Kate had so resented as a child, but which now she found oddly warming.

After the impersonal, couldn't-care-less attitude of the busy shops in London, it was almost pleasant to be in a place where one was known and welcomed.

'Hear you've brought your daughter back with you. A right bonny girl by all accounts. And her dad . . .'

'Cherry's father isn't and never has been a part of our lives,' Kate told her firmly. She had never lied about the circumstances of Cherry's birth, and she wasn't going to start now.

She almost felt the rustle of speculation run round the small, enclosed space, but she refused

to give in to the urge to turn her head and see
how the other people in the queue behind her
had received her information.

'Aye, well, there's many a woman who would
like to be able to say the same thing,' Susan
Edmonson replied placidly, adding with a
wryness that brought several chuckles from the
other women waiting to be served, 'And some
days it's easy to see why.'

Since her own husband was one of the most
henpecked males in existence, Kate herself only
just managed to stop herself from smiling.

She left the post office, head held high, feeling
as though she had just emerged triumphant
from an ordeal.

Times had changed, of course. Even up here
there were now girls rearing their children alone,
but even so, for her parents' sake if nothing else,
she wanted to re-establish herself creditably in
the village.

As she turned to close the door behind her,
she heard Susan Edmonson murmuring confid-
ingly to her next customer, 'Clever girl she was,
too. A schoolteacher now. Still, these things
happen. And what I always say is that it's the
innocent ones that get caught out.'

This latter comment was added in a virtuous
tone that made Kate grin a little.

The sun had come out, and she had to shade
her eyes from its glare as she made to cross the
road and return to the Land Rover. She was
thirsty; the heat of the sun was penetrating the
sweatshirt she was wearing and making her

wish she had put on something cooler. The pub
beckoned, but she suspected that up here in the
Dales it was still not totally accepted for a young
woman to walk into a pub on her own, and so
she contented herself by promising herself a
glass of her mother's home-made lemonade
once she reached the farm. She herself had
remembered the recipe and made the drink for
Cherry, but somehow it never tasted quite the
same.

Sighing faintly, she stepped out into the road,
only to come to an abrupt halt as a Range Rover
swept round the corner, surely travelling at a
faster speed than was safe. She had a
momentary glimpse of the driver: a hawkish
male profile, set mouth that looked rather grim,
thick, very dark hair, a brown forearm emerging
from the stark whiteness of a short-sleeved shirt,
and then the world spun dizzyingly out of focus,
and she barely registered the dark blue
paintwork or the initials of the government body
stamped boldly on the Range Rover bodywork in
white, because time had spun backwards and
she was left feeling as though she had suddenly
walked into the past.

That man driving the Range Rover had been so
like Silas. An older Silas, of course. A harder
Silas. She shivered, reproaching herself for her
carelessness in stepping off the pavement and
her idiocy in allowing her memories to have such
a powerful effect upon her that she was actually
seeing Silas in the features of a stranger.

CHAPTER THREE

'ARE you all right?'

The arm that went round to support her made Kate stiffen, the unfamiliar but friendly male voice in her ear making her swivel in shock.

She found herself looking into a pair of friendly blue eyes in a face that was ruggedly attractive rather than handsome.

An untidy mop of brown hair, bleached blond by the sun, added an almost boyish appeal to a man whom she suspected was somewhere around her own age.

He was wearing the Daleman's uniform of worn tweed jacket, checked shirt, and brogues, although in his case worn jeans had replaced her father's generation of Dalesmen's twill trousers.

'I promise you, I'm quite safe,' he told her, feeling her tense withdrawal and moving his arm until he was only steadying her.

His fingers felt slightly rough where they touched her wrist. He had reached out instinctively to grab her as she had stepped off the pavement, Kate recognised, and she gave him a faint smile.

'I don't bite, kick or stamp!' he added with a grin. 'I leave that kind of thing to my patients. I'm with the local veterinary practice,' he added when she didn't respond to his joke. 'Tim Stepping.'

He released her to hold out his hand and shake her own. He had a handshake that was pleasant without being aggressive, and now that her shock was fading, Kate remembered her manners and smiled warmly at him.

It was like watching the sun chase the clouds across the Dales, he thought in bemused appreciation. She was one of the most lovely women he had ever seen: as delicate and fragile-looking as an orchid with her pale skin and lovely colouring, and yet at the same time he sensed a strength about her that intrigued him.

She had the stamp of the Dales on her and yet she was different: more sophisticated, more glossy, with that immaculate haircut, and hands that felt soft and smooth. And yet, for all her sophistication, there was an air of vulnerability about her.

'Kate Seton,' Kate responded.

'Seton?' His eyebrows rose. 'Not John Seton's daughter?'

'The very same,' Kate responded lightly, wondering how much gossip he had heard about her.

John Seton's daughter . . . Well, that would explain both the sophistication and the vulnerability. He glanced betrayingly over his shoulder, and Kate said drily, 'My daughter is at the farm.'

His tanned skin flushed slightly, and he apologised. 'I'm sorry, that was crass of me.'

'Not at all,' Kate said brittly.

Suddenly her self-confidence had deserted her, and she knew that it was not because of this pleasant, fair-haired man who was looking at her now like one of her father's pups when it had been smacked, but because of the dark-haired man driving the Range Rover. How idiotic could she be, reacting like this to the sight of an unknown man? Heavens, she must have seen hundreds of dark-haired men during her years in London, and yet not one of them had affected her like that.

'I'm coming up to your father's place later on today. He's got a ewe he wants me to look at.'

'My daughter will be pleased,' Kate told him, trying to make amends. 'It's the ambition of her life to become a vet, so I warn you now, she'll probably pester you to death.'

She made to cross the road, amused and touched by the way that he walked with her, almost as though guarding her.

'Are you sure you're OK to drive this thing?' he asked her, eyeing her tiny frame and the heavy bulk of the Land Rover. 'That was quite a daydream you must have been in, to step off the pavement like that.'

'Whoever was driving that Range Rover was driving far too fast,' Kate defended. Inside, she was holding her breath and deriding herself at the same time. Why not simply ask him if he knew who had been driving it, instead of fishing so stupidly?

'I didn't see the driver,' Tim admitted, 'but it was one of the vehicles from the government experimental station.'

'Do you go there much?' Kate asked him.

He shook his head.

'No, they have their own resident vets. They're

doing research into animal diseases that sometimes requires them all to go into quarantine—no
one allowed in or out—and outsiders aren't
encouraged at any time. Very wise, probably, in
view of the potential danger. I suspect they're
trying to find an antidote for rabies, but that's only
my own private feeling. And then, of course,
there's the continued problem of assessing the
radiation fall-out from Chernobyl . . .'

'All that on one fifteen-hundred-acre estate,'
Kate marvelled sardonically, but Tim shook his
head again.

'Don't knock it. They're doing one hell of a
valuable job, and unlike some of the big phar-
maceutical companies, their research isn't at the
mercy of shareholders and profit margins. Some of
the villagers seem to think they're testing bombs in
there, but they couldn't be more wrong. If only the
people in there were allowed to announce it . . .'

His words gave Kate food for thought. Her
father had told her that the establishment of the
research station had caused resentment in the
village, and despite the value of the work it was
engaged on Kate suspected that that resentment
would probably only increase if the local farming
community suspected the station was engaged in
experiments with rabies and other dangerous,
contagious diseases.

She arrived back in time to help her mother after
lunch, wondering how she could best broach the
subject of the man in the Range Rover. To describe
him physically to her mother was bound to elicit
too much curiosity, and yet when she sketchily

drew a verbally toned-down image of him when describing the incident, her mother shook her head and told her, 'I haven't met anyone from the station—they don't mix locally. They even shop outside the area. It must be an odd sort of life, living in a community and yet separate from it,' she added musingly.

Of course, there was no earthly chance that the man could have been Silas, but even so it disturbed Kate to know that there was any man in the neighbourhood so powerfully like her memories of him that even thinking about the incident now made her stomach churn. Odd that she could so easily forgive her father, and yet still feel so bitterly resentful of the way Silas had treated her. Perhaps because her father's betrayal had been born of love and Silas's of callous indifference.

After lunch, Cherry insisted on returning to the paddocks with her grandfather, and having assured herself that she was not going to overtire herself Kate allowed her to go, noticing as she did so the healthy glow that being outside had already given Cherry's skin.

She had brought some work with her—assignments she wanted to prepare for the new school term—and she took her work upstairs to her room so that she could concentrate on it.

Kate loved teaching, which was odd, really, for she had never intended to go into it. Research had been her chosen field—library work; and yet she now acknowledged that, despite its constant heartaches and strains, teaching gave her considerable pleasure. She was lucky in being at a school where the parents were caring and concerned, the children mostly from immigrant families, who were keen to see their offspring succeed in the world, and who saw education as a passport to that success.

Children up here in the Dales came from families with a similar respect for education, although the children often had to travel many miles to get to school. The local village school no longer existed, and if she and Cherry moved . . .

Her heart thudded uncomfortably. Slow down, Kate cautioned herself . . . They were here on holiday, that was all. And yet, as she stood up and looked out of her window, she acknowledged that her soul had been starved for the sight of her home. She missed its grandeur and its freedom; London caged and imprisoned her, although she hadn't realised how much until now. But coming home would mean such an upheaval. She would have to find somewhere to live . . .

'Kate . . .'

The anxiety in her mother's voice as she called to her took her hurrying to the top of the stairs.

'Annabel's gone,' her mother told her worriedly. 'Could you go and look for her? I'm right in the middle of baking.'

Annabel was the latest in a long line of nanny-goats her mother insisted on keeping, despite their destructive tendencies, for she claimed that their milk was far healthier than that from cows. As Kate went downstairs in response to her mother's summons, she learned that Annabel had chewed through her tether and wandered off.

'If she gets into the government place, there'll be such trouble,' her mother worried. 'There was such a to-do the other week. Some group or other broke in . . . They're very security conscious.'

'I'll go and look for her. She can't have gone far,' Kate reassured her, knowing the breed's penchant for stopping to eat whatever took its fancy.

She suspected she would find the animal less than a few yards down the lane, but she discovered that she was wrong, and she had walked as far as the boundary of her father's land with that now owned by the experimental station before she realised she was wrong.

Surely Annabel couldn't have strayed in there? she reflected, gazing at the high, heavy fencing that reared unattractively above the mellow stone walls that bounded the estate.

Worn stone steps set into the wall showed where there had once been access over it, and Kate climbed up them so that she could look into the enclosed grounds.

To her horror, she saw that the goat had indeed strayed inside the perimeter. She looked up when Kate called her name, but refused to move, simply shaking her silky white head and continuing her meal.

How on earth had she got in? Kate wondered wryly. Agile as the creature was, she couldn't have climbed over the wall and the perpendicular fence.

She scrambled back down the wal, jumping the last couple of feet, and acknowledging as her muscles protested that she was slightly out of condition. Time was when she would have done that without having to soothe scraped palms of too-tender, 'citified' skin.

Realising that she would have to find out where the goat had got in and get her out again, she looked to her left and right, wondering which direction to take first. Then she spotted some of the goat's droppings, and with a faint sigh of relief turned to the right.

A narrow, unkempt lane ran alongside the boundary wall, leading to a farm which had been empty for almost two years following the death of its owner, an incomer into the area who had tried and failed to raise prize cattle on the exposed fellsides. The farm had recently been sold, according to her father, but no one knew to whom. Her father had been slightly disgruntled by the sale, since he had wanted to purchase the land himself. Although not suitable for cattle, it could be used for sheep.

Kate had come out in thin-soled shoes, and the sharp stones in the unmade-up road struck painfully through them. Cursing under her breath, Kate bent to rub her foot, and then straightened up, her pain forgotten as her attention was caught by bright scraps of metal among the tufts of grass. As she walked over to examine them more closely, she realised that someone had cut through the boundary fence, and recently, too, and that it was here, where there was no protective wall to support it, that the goat had broken through. Sure enough, there were tufts of her white hair clinging to the wire.

Gingerly Kate pushed her own way through, wincing as the sharp barbs caught at her clothes, carefully pushing them to one side so that they didn't catch on her skin.

Even so, she couldn't avoid one barb escaping her hold and leaving a long and very painful scratch down her arm. Blood welled freely from it and she cursed her own carelessness. Her skin stung, but there was nothing she could do about it. Her primary concern now was to retrieve her mother's goat.

She had purposefully brought with her a pocket full of the pig nuts that the animal apparently adored, and as she walked carefully down towards it she fished in her pocket and removed some of them, hoping that once Annabel caught the scent of them she would follow her docilely back on to their own land.

Annabel caught the scent of them, and dutifully came trotting up to her, but Kate had forgotten the breed's wiliness, and wasn't prepared for the goat butting her. She lost her balance and fell over, the nuts scattering.

By the time she had regained her balance, Annabel had eaten the lot and was standing skittishly several yards away from her.

Unwisely, Kate lost her patience and gave chase.

Ten minutes later, hot and out of breath, she acknowledged defeat. She was going to have to go home and get one of her father's men to help her.

Her body ached where she had fallen, and her arm stung, dried blood clinging to her skin. She had a blister on one heel, and all in all she felt extremely irritated and uncomfortable. Limping painfully, she headed back to the gap in the fence.

The sound of something crashing heavily through the undergrowth behind her suddenly made her check. She looked round, saw nothing, and then her eyes widened as she focused disbelievingly on the body of the huge Alsatian launching itself at her.

Brought up on a farm she reacted instinctively, standing her ground and calling out sharply to the animal, 'Down!'

She saw it focus on her, mid-leap, its intelligent eyes registering its surprise at the command, but she had reacted too late to stop its weight landing on her and sending her sprawling to the ground beneath it.

Kate closed her eyes as she fell, the breath knocked from her lungs as she hit the hard earth, the undergrowth hardly cushioning the impact.

The dog landed squarely on top of her and pinned her there, and she opened her eyes to look at it.

It gave a tiny whine and she felt its feathery tail brush against her jean-covered legs.

Heartened by this sign of friendliness, Kate raised her arms to push it off, but instantly it growled, eyes rolling, lips pulling back to reveal strong, sharp teeth.

There were sounds of something else moving through the trees, although she wasn't sure what until she heard a man's voice saying curtly, 'Good dog, Max. Leave.'

As the dog moved off her, the man grabbed hold of her wrist and yanked her ungently to her feet.

'All right. Let's find out what's going on here . . .'

'Nothing's going on,' Kate told him shakily, noting the uniform he was wearing and the clipped military haircut. He was in his late fifties, she judged, but extremely fit; the kind of man one would prefer to have with one rather than against.

'I came in to fetch my mother's goat. There was a break in the fence.'

'Come on, you can do better than that. We know all about that break. Your lot made it the other night, and we've been waiting to see what you were going to do next. This way.'

Before Kate could protest he was practically frog-marching her away from the wall, and deeper into the grounds.

'What's going on? Where are you taking me?' Kate demanded angrily.

'To see the station head. We've had enough of you lot causing trouble. You've been warned, and you wouldn't listen, so this time we're taking tougher action.'

'You've got it all wrong,' Kate protested. 'I'm Kate Seton . . . My father farms next door. I'm not part of any group of saboteurs, no matter what you might think.' She felt his hesitation, and pressed, 'Look, all you've got to do is ring the farm and speak to my mother. She'll confirm what I'm saying. I came here looking for Annabel.'

'Annabel?' her captor demanded suspiciously.

'The goat,' Kate sighed.

At her side, the Alsatian whined, and without thinking she reached down to stroke him.

'Don't,' the man commanded, his ire giving way to astonishment as he saw the way the animal responded to her.

Although Kate had a healthy respect for them, she had no fear of dogs, and she had recognised instantly in the Alsatian a highly intelligent and well-trained beast whose instinct was not to harm.

'Damn thing,' she heard the man curse. 'I knew he was too soft for this business.'

'So why use him?' Kate asked, amused.

'Not my decision. The head of the station rescued him as a pup. He's his dog.' He saw the look in Kate's eyes and said defensively, 'We're getting proper guard-dogs in, but these things take time. Extra expenditure has to be sanctioned, and we didn't expect this kind of trouble up here. God, you'd think people would be grateful for what we're doing.'

'Maybe they would be, if they knew what it was,' Kate told him pointedly.

She was beginning to recover her self-confidence now. It was true that she had been caught in an embarrassing situation, and no doubt her father wouldn't be too pleased with her, but she had no doubts at all that once the station head had spoken to her mother, she would be released with a handsome apology.

After all, he was hardly likely to want to stir up local resentment by practically forcibly kidnapping the daughter of a respected local landowner.

The main building came in sight.

It hadn't changed much as far as Kate could see, although the overgrown gravel drive she remembered as a child had been weeded and cleaned.

As they walked in through the main entrance she marvelled at the faint, but unmistakable antiseptic scent that hung on the air. It even smelled like a government building, she acknowledged, and fell to wondering how much of the stuff they must buy and from where; her reverie abruptly halted as she was escorted into a room filled with the clutter of filing cabinets and other office paraphernalia.

A young man was frowning over a VDU screen. He looked up in some surprise when he saw Kate, and began uncertainly, 'I'm sorry, but . . .'

'I caught her trespassing,' her captor interrupted him. 'She claims she was looking for her mother's goat. I thought the boss ought to see her. Especially in view of you know what . . .'

Despite the fierce mien of her captor, Kate couldn't help being amused by the meaningful look he gave the young man, and her sense of humour, so often her downfall in the past, led her into trouble now, as she teased, tongue-in-cheek, not thinking of the potential consequences.

'There's no need to be so secretive. I know all about the rabies research.'

'Oh, do you now?'

'The curt male voice behind her made her freeze. Not because of the shock of realising that someone else had entered the room, but because of its distant familiarity.

Time was distilled so that she was conscious of every fragment of it; every nuance of what hearing that voice meant; every carefully placed piece fate had set in the jigsaw puzzle of her life.

She couldn't for the life of her turn round. She felt him move, and felt the frisson of sensation shock through her as he did, and she felt the breath of his words against the nape of her neck as she ducked her head to avoid recognition.

'Who exactly is this, Tom?'

'I found her trespassing right by the cut in the fence. She claimed she was looking for her mother's goat. She says she's John Seton's daughter.'

'Does she now? Well, let's have a look and see, shall we?'

The silky menace in his voice warned her of what to expect. Kate lifted her head proudly and turned to look at him.

Recognition, powerful and painful, arched between them. She saw his jaw tauten briefly, and it was left to her to say quietly, 'Hello, Silas.'

She felt the shock of her words reverberate around the room.

'Kate . . .' He acknowledged her tersely with a brief inclination of his head. 'I heard you were back.'

And had he heard about Cherry as well? Very probably. Her mouth thinned and, seeing it, he felt an intense weariness settle on him.

Once, this woman had meant so much to him.

So very much, but she had walked out on him virtually without a word, and since coming to the Dales he had learned that she was living with her daughter in London.

He wondered about the man who shared her life . . . who had given her her child, and was disturbed to discover that the old pain was far more than a mere echo. To cover his feelings he said grimly, 'What the devil were you playing at? You must know that this estate is private land.'

'I've told you. I was looking for my mother's goat. She'd escaped, and I found that she'd strayed in. All I was trying to do was to get her back.'

Suddenly she felt both tired and tearful. Her body ached from its impact with the ground. The scratch on her arm stung, and as she raised it instinctively trying to ease the pain, she saw Silas frown.

'When did you do that?' he demanded sharply.

'I caught it on the wire,' she responded absently. A smear of soil clung to it and, seeing it, Silas exclaimed sharply to his assistant, 'Go and get some sterile dressings, will you please, Sam? Tom, have you checked to find this damn goat? We can't have it roaming about . . .'

'If it exists,' her captor said sarcastically.

'She does exist,' Kate retorted, stung by his disbelief. 'Her name's Annabel. Look, all you have to do to confirm everything I've said is to ring my mother. As a matter of fact, I'd like to speak to her anyway. She'll be getting concerned.'

'You can speak to her later, when I've made one

or two things clear to you.'

Silas turned his back on her and stared out of the window. There was an odd atmosphere in the room, and when he turned back he addressed not Kate herself but her guard.

'Sam, am I right in thinking we've no spare rooms at the moment?'

'Yes, we're on full strength. You said yourself we'd need to run all the tests . . .'

'Yes, I know.'

'Look, I want to leave,' Kate interrupted them angrily.

'I'm afraid you can't.'

Can't? She stared at Silas, not believing what she was hearing. It was a joke . . . a sick, cruel joke. It had to be.

He saw her face and said quietly, 'We're in the middle of experiments here that necessitate all of us remaining in quarantine for at least another week.'

'No! No, that's not true. I saw you myself . . . driving through the village this morning.'

'I'd gone to pick up some supplies that had been left for us at a pre-arranged spot. I didn't come into contact with anyone, and even that was a risk. I'm afraid there's no alternative. Until after the quarantine period ends, you'll have to stay here. And so will Annabel,' he said with a brief smile, adding frowningly, 'if we can find her, which I hope to God we can. We don't want her getting back out of the estate, Tom. You'd better get the men and go and gather . . .'

'Wait!' Kate protested as her captor turned to

leave, her inbred instincts making her overcome her shock and fear to reach into her pocket and remove the remaining pig nuts.

'Take these. She loves them, apparently.'

And then Tom was gone and they were alone, apart from the Alsatian, Max, who was lying heavily on her feet. Guarding her—hardly—she reflected wryly as she looked down at the dog and he responded with a heavy beat of his tail.

'I'll deal with that cut and then I'll take you to your room. I'm sorry about this, but it's necessary.'

He had regained control of himself now and was trying to treat her as he would have treated any strange woman in the same situation.

'I think I can deal with a simple graze myself,' she told him, frightened by what she had heard, despite her determination not to show it.

'Very probably so,' Silas said quietly. 'But it may not be just a simple graze, and so I'd prefer to attend to it myself.'

His words reverberated through her head, and she stared at him in shock.

'You're not trying to say that I could have rabies, are you?' she whispered, uttering the fear that crawled along her spine and left a vile taste in her mouth.

'Rabies?' He frowned. 'No, not that . . . But we are conducting other experiments here on animal diseases, and we can't take the risk that something you might have touched could be contaminated and that you could have carried that contamination into an open wound by touching it.'

He picked up the telephone on his desk and pushed the instrument towards her.

'You'll want to speak to your mother. I should warn her that you'll be here for at least a week.'

'A week?' Her lips trembled. 'But I can't. Cherry . . .'

Cherry would be perfectly safe with her grandparents, she told herself stoutly, and the last thing she must do was to break down in front of this cold-eyed man who had once been her lover, who was the father of her child.

What mischievous and devious twist of fate had brought them together again like this? And how clever and all-knowing her subconscious must be to have recognised him so easily. And her body to have reacted to that recognition? She shivered tensely, not wanting to remember that frisson of acute loss that had rushed over her when she had seen him at the wheel of the Range Rover. He would never be hers and he never had been. He was married to another woman, had children with her, had deliberately kept her in ignorance of those commitments. He was a man to be despised, not desired.

'You'll want to speak to your husband as well, of course.'

Kate stared at him, and then, with her head held high, said proudly, 'I have no husband.'

CHAPTER FOUR

NO HUSBAND. The words bounced against Silas's skull as he listened to her speaking to her mother, explaining with commendable calm what had happened. She had always been strong, even though she herself probably didn't realise it. Strong and yet so very, very female, and he had loved her to the point of distraction.

But to her he had simply been a diversion. He shouldn't blame her too much. She had been so young, and he surely old enough to realise that and not to have tried to tie her down.

Had he not pressed her into that commitment, not insisted on that engagement, would she perhaps have stayed?

Kate replaced the receiver. Any moment now she would turn and look at him. He composed his features into a hard mask. She had changed so little; she was, if anything, even more beautiful as a woman than she had been as a teenager.

Her mother had assured her that she would make sure that Cherry didn't worry. Her daughter was sensible enough to be told the bare outline of why the quarantine was necessary. Cherry was an intelligent child, and Kate had never made the mistake of underestimating her intelligence nor of talking down to her.

The door opened and Sam came back, empty-handed. 'We've used the last of the sterile stuff. I remembered when I went to get it that the new supply is in the boxes you collected this morning, and they aren't unpacked yet.'

'It doesn't matter. I've got some at my place. Kate will have to stay there, anyway. It's the only place where there's any spare room.'

'I am not staying with *you*,' Kate told him furiously, the moment his assistant disappeared.

'You don't have any alternative,' he told her grimly. 'And even if you had, are you honestly telling me that you'd prefer to share a dormitory and a bathroom with a dozen or so men rather than having your own private room?'

Of course she wouldn't, and if she only dared let herself acknowledge it, her traitorous heart would like nothing better than to be close to Silas again. But such traitorous impulses couldn't be allowed to have life. Silas was a married man, and she was a woman who had already borne him one illegitimate child.

Kate shivered. Put like that, the silent words fell harshly against her conscience, but those were the facts, harsh and unpleasant though they might be.

'Exactly how long will this quarantine have to last?' she asked him coldly, pushing aside her personal vulnerabilities and presenting him with an unreadable face.

What had happened to the joyous girl he had known? he wondered, mourning her. That girl had been a creature of quicksilver emotions, each one of them vividly illuminating her face. He remembered how she had looked at him that first time he had made love to her, and a terrible sense of loss and despair he thought he had long put behind him surfaced through the barriers he had imposed against it, threatening his self-control.

He turned away so that she wouldn't see it, and Kate, mistaking the gesture for one of bored irritation with her questions, compressed her mouth. She had every right to ask these questions and to get answers to them.

'How long?' she pressed.

'I've already told you—a week.'

She was aghast.

'I can't stay here for a week!'

'I'm afraid you'll have to,' Silas told her quietly.

'And if I don't choose to?'

This was the Kate he remembered, her eyes flashing warning signs, her chin tilted in feminine rejection of his right to impose his will on her.

'Then I have the power to make you,' he told her equably. 'This is a government establishment, and I'm in charge. For God's sake,' he demanded, suddenly losing his temper, 'do you think I want you here?'

She had known he wouldn't, of course, but hearing the words thrown at her in that angry, bitter voice hurt. She turned away, fighting to control the surge of hot, burning tears that stung her eyes, her teeth digging sharply into her bottom lip, leaving tiny indentations when she had to release it.

Silas stared at them, mesmerised by the neatly incised marks and the memories they aroused.

Once, in the early days before they had been

lovers, he had inflicted similar wounds to those, driven almost out of his mind with desire for her, and yet at the same time not wanting to push her into full sexuality before she was ready. She had cried out beneath his mouth, pushing against his chest, and he had soothed the pain he had inflicted with the moist balm of his tongue until both of them forgot that his caress was supposed to be merely comforting and she had gone wild in his arms, covering his face with frantic little kisses and his mouth with hungry little bites.

He pulled himself back to the present, angry at his own vulnerability.

'I'll show you where you'll be staying,' he told her curtly. 'And we'll get that scratch attended to at the same time.'

Still not ready to give up, Kate retaliated acidly, 'I take it that during this incarceration, I'll at least have access to a telephone.'

'There is one at the house. I'll get someone to put an extension into your room for you. It's this way.'

Without a word Kate turned on her heel and followed him through the main hall and down a maze of passages which ended in a grim, old-fashioned kitchen, dimly lit by a too-small window.

Remembering the gracious proportions of the rest of the house, Kate marvelled at the conditions in which the ordinary person had once been expected to work.

The kitchen was obviously in use. A huge freezer had been installed and a modern cooker, plus two microwave ovens.

A young man was busily chopping vegetables as they walked through. He smiled at Silas and then stared at Kate, plainly astonished to see her.

'Mrs . . .' Silas began.

'Miss Seton,' Kate interrupted him curtly, as he turned to introduce her. She saw him frown and check, but then, as though remembering their audience, he continued, 'Miss Seton trespassed into the grounds in pursuit of a goat, and so I'm afraid she's going to have to be incarcerated here for the rest of the quarantine period . . . Larry is our chef,' he explained unnecessarily to Kate.

'It's beef stew tonight,' Larry told her with a grin. 'There's a smashing herb garden outside and . . .'

'And I hope you haven't been using any of them,' Silas cautioned him, turning to explain to Kate, 'We're conducting several agricultural experiments here, and one of them involves testing new fertilisers, hence the ban on eating anything in the grounds.' He opened the back door and stood by it, waiting for her.

Kate dutifully followed him out across the cobbled yard and past the now empty stables.

'The rest of the staff are living up there,' Silas told her, indicating the area above the stables with a brief jerk of his head.

'Why not in the house?' Kate questioned him.

'Too much damp in the upper rooms, and, like all other government schemes in their infancy, we're operating on something of a shoestring.'

Beyond the stables was a paddock filled with

sheep of a similar breed to her father's, only these had fleeces that were much thicker, surely?

'New experimental breed,' Silas told her noticing her interest. 'We're going to overwinter them on the fells to test their endurance ability. They carry twenty per cent more wool than the best rivals; they're more resistant to disease.'

As she walked past them, the man who had first discovered her in the grounds came running up. 'We've found the goat and isolated it,' he told Silas.

'Good. I'll show Miss Seton to her room, and then we'd better decide what we're going to do about that gap in the fence. I'd hoped our midnight visitors would have returned by now, but we can't take the risk of waiting for them any longer. We don't want anyone or anything else finding their way through that gap.'

Curious in spite of herself, Kate asked impulsively, 'But who would want to break in and why? If you are working on animal vaccines, it's so very worth while.'

'Powerful drugs of any kind have to be tested,' Silas told her quietly. 'It's an unfortunate fact of life that sometimes this means that they have to be tested on animals—not always with happy results. Here we keep such testings to the absolute minimum.

'It's an extremely vexed question, but I sometimes think our protesters might be better directing their endeavours against the many thousands of people who mistreat their household pets, or far worse—their children.'

He started walking again, following a rutted and overgrown lane that ran towards what she vaguely remembered as being the rear exit to the estate.

Less than half a mile down it was a solid, square, stone house surrounded by its own patch of garden.

'It's a dower house of some kind,' Silas told her, 'built probably in the mid-eighteen-hundreds.'

Kate hesitated outside it, absently noting how the garden had grown wild and how bleak the uncurtained windows appeared, and yet it was a pleasant enough place.

'Won't your wife mind you inflicting me on her like this?' she asked him uncomfortably. Panic hit her. It had been one thing for him to tell her that she would have to share his home. It was another to come face to face with the realisation that she would be living side by side with Silas's wife.

He froze and then turned to stare at her, and said harshly, 'What wife? I'm not married.' And the shadow of some remembered pain quite clearly clouded his features, rendering him achingly vulnerable, if only briefly.

She had never seen vulnerability in him before, but was it just as she had never seen love and anguish in her father—because she had been too young to want to see? She had practically hero-worshipped Silas, her love still tinged with the fantasy of a teenager's romantic dreams. She had put him on a pedestal and had wanted him to stay there, she recognised with adult perception. Now he had well and truly fallen from that pedestal.

What had happened to that dark-haired, laughing woman? Had she discovered his infidelity and divorced him?

'I'm sorry.'

She wasn't quite sure why she made the trite apology, but she didn't expect his face to darken the way it did, nor his body to tense as though in mortal pain as he said savagely, 'So am I.'

And then he was walking away from her, his lithe body suddenly oddly uncoordinated.

Whatever had happened, he must still love that woman; nothing else could account for that haunting look of pain in his eyes. So why the affair with her? She shivered, recognising her own pain, a pain that came with the knowledge that she herself had meant so little to him, and certainly nothing to compare with the woman who caused his eyes to cloud with pain and his body to tense.

'Are you coming inside or are you going to stay out there all day?' he demanded harshly.

He had unlocked the door and was waiting for her to precede him inside.

The house was as dreary inside as it had appeared from out; the large, square sitting-room could have been pleasant, but the leather chesterfield and the furniture were covered by a thin film of dust, the room bare of colour and life. It was drab and dull, in fact. Was that because Silas didn't have time to make it any different, or because it reflected the way he felt about himself and his life?

What had happened to his sons? she wondered, resenting the pain she was causing herself, but knowing as a parent the agony he must feel at being separated from them. Already, even knowing that Cherry would be happy and safe with her parents, she ached to be with her daughter.

She glanced at the phone and, as though he read her mind, Silas said harshly, 'Worrying about what he's going to say, are you?'

He? She refused to respond to the taunt. Let him think what he liked.

'The kitchen's through here,' he told her curtly, pushing open another door.

It was as drab as the sitting-room; as was the dining-room and the room he was using as a study.

Upstairs the house had four bedrooms, but only one bathroom. The bath must be the original Victorian one, Kate suspected; the water, Silas told her, was heated by an immersion, and since he virtually only slept in the house and it was summer, he made do with an electric heater whenever it was cold.

Looking round the drab bareness, Kate wondered what on earth she was going to do with herself, quarantined here for a week.

How often had she groaned for time to herself, for privacy and space, but now that she had them, she couldn't think how on earth she was going to fill the empty time.

She felt more alone and deserted than she had ever felt in her life.

'I'll need clothes . . . toothbrush . . . . my work,' she told him stiffly, refusing to look at him in case he guessed her feelings.

'Someone will have to leave them outside the main gates. No one's allowed in. You must see why,' he added in a more gentle tone, and she had a sudden vision of Cherry, and knew beyond doubt that for the sake of her daughter's safety she would spend three times as long here if it was necessary. 'I'll get that phone extension fixed up for you, but in the meantime, feel free to use the one in my study. First, though, I want to attend to that scratch.'

There was a very utilitarian bathroom cabinet in the room, and he opened it, extracting cotton wool, lint, a bottle of clear fluid and an unmarked tube.

It wasn't until he washed his hands and then turned briskly towards her that Kate realised he intended to clean the scratch himself.

'I can do it,' she told him hastily.

Grim-faced, he watched her back off from him. So even the thought of him touching her repulsed her now, did it? A muscle flickered in his jaw and, seeing it, Kate hesitated. She was behaving like a child, terrified of his touch in case it awakened sensations she wouldn't be able to control; but she wasn't a girl of eighteen any more, she was a woman. Moreover, she was a woman whose sexual urges had remained dormant for over ten years. It was hardly likely that the clinical touch of a man cleaning her skin was likely to reduce her to a trembling physical need, was it?

'I'll get Graham, our resident doctor, to come and check you over later, but it's unlikely that you will have contracted anything. However, quarantine rules must be obeyed.'

He was trying to reassure her, Kate recognised, and she wondered at his kindness, wishing bitterly he had not evinced it. It would make it so much easier for her if she could despise him as a man as well as a lover.

But she didn't despise him, she acknowledged, as he swabbed her arm with the cleaning fluid and she fought not to flinch, not because of its mild sting but because of the sensation of his fingers against her skin.

She looked away as he cleaned the scratch thoroughly, every muscle locked in desperate despair.

She felt him smear on the ointment and then wrap her arm in lint.

'I'll look at it again tonight, but I don't think there's going to be any problem. Does it hurt at all?'

'Not as much as the bruises I got when I fell,' Kate told him drily.

She saw him frown, and for one appalling moment she actually thought he was going to demand to see them, but to her relief he simply recapped the ointment and carried it back to the cupboard.

'I've got to get back to my office, but please make yourself at home. There's a freezer in the kitchen if you want something to eat.

'We only get the luxury of fresh supplies once a month, but tonight you're in luck. I'll bring them back with me later.'

'Don't you eat with the others?' Kate asked

him, curious suddenly about his life. Surely it must be a very lonely existence. Had the loss of his wife turned him into a man who preferred solitude to the company of others?

'Not normally. I'm head of station,' he reminded her. 'It can be inhibiting for them to have me around during their leisure time, especially if they want to let off steam.'

'Don't you ever get lonely?'

She had asked the question impulsively, bitterly regretting having done so when he gave her a level look and said quietly, 'I got used to that a long time ago.'

When his wife had left?

Suddenly she needed desperately to hear Cherry's bright voice, but she waited until he had gone before returning to his study and picking up the receiver.

She felt like an intruder here in the room where he worked, and yet there was no reason why she should. There were no personal touches about the room, no photographs on the desk, nothing at all to give someone who didn't know him any clues about the kind of man he was.

Her mother answered the phone, and quickly brought Cherry to speak to Kate. Wryly, Kate realised that her daughter had had no time to miss her; she was full of her morning's activities, and how she had helped her grandfather with his dogs. In addition to the supposedly untrainable Laddie, it seemed there was also a litter of puppies just over six months old and ready to start learning their trade.

'Gramps has given me one of my own to train, and next year, if he does really well, I'm going to enter for the beginners' class.'

Kate was astonished. The pups weren't pets, but extremely valuable working-dogs, and it was unheard of for her father to allow anyone other than himself to have anything to do with their training. As Kate recalled it, he even supervised their diets.

'He says I've got a natural skill with them,' Cherry boasted, 'but then, so I should have. I'm a Seton.'

Kate's laughter caught in her throat. Hearing the proud note in Cherry's voice, she recognised that, for all she had so much of her father in her, Cherry had something of her grandfather as well. She wondered ruefully if her father had realised yet that Cherry had also inherited some of his stubbornness.

She wasn't blind. She knew quite well that the pup was her father's way of ensuring that they would keep returning to the Dales, and yet she couldn't find it in her heart to blame him for half bribing her daughter. Part of her acknowledged her understanding of why he should do so, and the scar caused by his original anger and rejection faded just a little more. Her father loved Cherry and Cherry loved him, and she herself was not going to spoil the relationship growing between them out of her own bitter memories. At least Cherry would be getting to know her grandparents while she was shut up here, Kate thought, closing her mind to the irony of the fact that *she* would be unwillingly close to Cherry's father.

She explained about the quarantine, trying to soothe the quick alarm in her daughter's voice.

'It's all right darling . . . now, don't worry. Grandma and Grandpa will look after you, and when I come home you'll be able to show me how well you've trained your pup. I'll be able to speak to you every day, and when Gramps brings my clothes he can bring your photograph with him.'

She chatted for a few more minutes until she heard the happy, confident note re-enter Cherry's voice. Before asking to speak to her father, she said quietly, 'I love you very much.'

Tears stung her eyes as she waited for Cherry to fetch her father. She didn't bother to check them, letting them fall because there was no need to hide how she felt now. And then she heard a sound behind her.

Silas was standing in the doorway, his face hard and bitter.

When had he come back, and why? Horribly conscious of her tears and the disadvantage of her position, Kate dashed the drops away with impatient fingers.

'I'd forgotten that there's no spare bedding. I've arranged for some to be brought down for you,' Silas told her harshly.

He was looking at her as though he wanted to kill her, Kate recognised shiveringly. What had she done to merit such a look, or was it simply that seeing her had brought home to him all that he had lost . . . all that his brief affair with her must have cost him?

In another man she might have pitied him, but how could she pity someone who had deceived her as he had, who had allowed her to believe he loved her, that he was to *free* to love her?

She turned back to the phone and her father, explaining the situation to him, and asking him if he could bring her clothes and other necessities to the main entrance of the estate.

When she replaced the receiver, Silas had gone.

'Well, there doesn't seem to be anything wrong there.'

Graham Crew was a large cheerful man in his early forties, who had examined Kate's arm and her bruises with a gentleness belied by his physical appearance.

'I expect Silas has already told you why we have to take the precaution of keeping you here, but there's really nothing to worry about,' he told her comfortingly. 'You'll be perfectly safe.'

'Silas seemed concerned that I might have picked up some kind of contamination from the soil.'

'Was he? It's possible, but highly unlikely. To tell the truth, we need to keep you here not so much for your own safety, but for the protection of the animals and livestock in the dale.

'We have beasts here undergoing treatment. Someone broke in the other night and managed to free one of them. Luckily we found him and he was still on the estate, but we can't risk either you or your goat carrying infection outside.'

He frowned as he got up.

'I can't understand why Silas doesn't do something with this place. It's all right for the rest of us, most of us are creatures of passage, so to speak, but he's been here right from the start. Perhaps you can do something about it while you're here. It needs . . .'

'A woman's touch?' Kate supplied wryly.

He grinned at her. 'All right, so I'm an old-fashioned chauvinist. It's quite permissible at my age, or at least that's what I tell my wife and daughter. So far, I haven't managed to convince them.'

He got up. 'Will we be having the pleasure of your company at dinner tonight, or is Silas going to be selfish and keep you to himself? I know what would be my choice,' he added with another grin.

Kate couldn't help liking him, and they were laughing together five minutes later when Silas came in. He scowled at both of them and disappeared in the direction of his study.

Cherry had been banned from accompanying her father to the estate gates, which was just as well, Kate reflected as she battled with foolish tears when she saw her father.

'All this fuss for an idiotic goat,' he growled, but Kate could see that he was relieved to see that she was all right, and for his sake she put on a cheerful smile and made a couple of joking remarks.

'A week will soon pass for me. I'm not so sure how you and Mum are going to feel after a week of Cherry.'

'Don't you worry about the lass,' he told Kate, his face softening. 'We'll see she's all right. It's a rare treat to watch her with the dogs. Got a flair for it, she has.'

'She's determined she's going to have that pup ready for next year's junior trials,' Kate warned him.

'Aye.' His face softened again. 'I reckon she'll do it, an' all.'

After he had gone, one of the men, dressed from head to foot in protective clothing, went outside to collect her things.

In the privacy of her room she unpacked them. Right on the top of her suitcase was Cherry's photograph. She hugged it to her and then studied her daughter's smiling face. Whatever else it had cost her, her relationship with Silas had given her this. She propped the frame up on the bedside table and then started to unpack her clothes. She would have to find out about proper washing facilities. There was no machine in Silas's kitchen, but presumably there must be something up at the main building.

Her mother had packed her schoolwork, and a huge box of fresh food, including some of her own home-made bread, Kate recognised.

The house was quiet, and she knew that she had it to herself. Silas would not want her company, of course; that went without saying. Was that why she could sense so much anger in him? Because he resented the way fate had tossed her back into his life? If so, his resentment could hardly equal hers.

Did he also share her fear? she wondered wryly. But then, why should he? He stood in no danger of their enforced proximity rekindling feelings he could never have experienced.

Was she really afraid of loving him again? She was older and surely wiser, no longer a young girl eager to believe that when a man said 'I love you', he meant it.

And yet the grim-faced man who had shown her up to this room and then stood back from her, his face shadowed and taut, a man who betrayed with every word he spoke about his work how strong his code of ethics was, was no careless philanderer.

But with her own eyes she had seen him take another woman into his arms, had heard her talk about their children.

'I have no wife,' he had told her bleakly, and yet she had felt no satisfaction, no pleasure in his very obvious pain. How unreliable human emotions were. How vulnerable human beings.

CHAPTER FIVE

KATE had dinner with those members of the establishment's work-force who were not on duty. A twenty-four-hour guard was being mounted on the premises; some of the experiments called for constant monitoring and the people who worked in the isolation unit ate alone, she was told by Silas's deputy, Sam Carter. Inevitably the talk turned to Silas himself.

'He lives for his work,' one of the men commented.

'Not entirely,' someone else pointed out. 'He's just bought that place, and I've heard a rumour that he's thinking of leaving here and turning himself into a farmer.'

As she listened, Kate discovered that Silas had bought a nearby farm, and she remembered him once telling her of his love of the land. It was something they had shared; only yesterday evening she had slipped away from the farmyard to take the familiar track that led upwards to the moorland . . .

Despite her active life, she was not as limber as she had been at eighteen, she reflected wryly, and her calf muscles had protested as she started to climb the steep incline. The chill evening breeze whipping off the fells had stung colour into her cheeks, her unconfined hair blowing out behind her like a dark red banner; her profile, as she turned just for a moment to look back the way she had come, outlined against the backdrop of fells and sky, pure and mediaeval.

How many times as a child she had walked that path, and in how many different moods.

As a teenager she had gone up there to gloat over the Seton kingdom spread out beneath her, and to dream daydreams of the times when Abbeydale still had its abbey and the road through the dale was busy with travellers. Elizabethan messengers had ridden through here carrying despatches from Scottish Mary to her cousin in England; Elizabeth's father's commissioners had sweated up this very incline on their fat donkeys as they went about the business of assessing the wealth of the churches. And way back before that, Richard III had sent urgent messages to his followers to rally them to his cause.

Later Kate's daydreams had taken a more practical turn as she bacame infected by the urgency of her need to break free of the confines of the dale. And she had broken free, but to what?

There had been those heady, delirious days of pleasure with Silas, a handful of weeks which had barely stretched into months. They had met in May.

Kate moved restlessly, not wanting to remember, but unable to stop herself thinking of how she had roamed the moorland in the long summer evenings, one of John Seton's dogs by her side. The ground was usually dry at the beginning of summer and she would sit there and think of him, the dog pressing into her side.

How much more conscious one was here of the vastness of the universe, its millions upon millions of stars shining overhead. Was there life out there . . . another world . . . another race?

She had met Silas at a debate on just that very subject. He, like her, had been in the audience; mesmerised by the power of the argument she had just heard, Kate had bumped into him as she got up to leave.

He had reached out to steady her, and even then, in her innocence of sex, she had been aware of the chemistry between them.

A mature student, he was completing a PhD course, having returned to take his degree after spending several years working his way around the world. He was twenty-six then, to her eighteen, an adult to her child; but it had been as a woman that she had reacted to him, on fire with the need that pulsed through her the moment he touched her.

He had smiled at her, as though he knew just what she was feeling; a warm, teasing smile that made her gaze in fascination at the full curve of his bottom lip and wonder with a sudden, hot rush of sensation what it would be like to have that very male mouth caressing her own.

In a daze she had heard him ask her something, realising almost too late that he was asking her if she would like to go for a drink.

Such was the casual way dates were made on campus, and she had had no hesitation at all in accepting.

And so it had begun. A shared drink at a pub in Lancaster favoured by students, a discussion which had seemed to embrace every subject under the sun, and yet of which later she could remember only him saying, 'Your eyes are the most remarkable colour. Like the sea at its very deepest point, dangerous and very, very alluring. A man could drown so easily in those green depths.'

And, with all the instincts of the woman emerging from the chrysalis of the girl-child, Kate had known and recognised the sexual power that emanated from him.

His eyes were tawny-gold, echoing the warmth of his skin, which was not Celtic pale like hers, but brushed with warm bronze as though he carried Latin blood in his veins.

He could well do so, he had told her. His family came from Cornwall, where sailors from the Spanish Armada had come ashore to mix their blood with those of the local population.

He had rarely talked to her about his family, a shutter coming down whenever the subject was mentioned. And no wonder, Kate thought tiredly.

Why had she never guessed that he might be married? She had accepted his sexual experience, his worldliness, without question, never even thinking that at twenty-six and already a man he might have a wife and family.

They had known one another six weeks before they made love. A long time in those permissive days, when her peers went quite happily to bed with boys they had known for less than six hours.

She had been nervous, timid and fearful, despite the fact that Silas knew she was still a virgin; frightened of not being able to match his sexual expertise, of disappointing him in some way.

He was living in a cottage some way out of Lancaster, and travelled to and from the university by car, a luxury outside the means of the majority of the students, and the rented cottage was a far cry from Kate's own shabby room on campus.

It was late June and the weather had still been hot. They had spent the previous two weekends together, and on each occasion she had been half expecting Silas to make love to her, half wanting him to and half dreading it.

She had been quite deliberately provocative with him in the way that only a naïve teenage girl could be, she remembered grimly, teasing him with come-on smiles and brief, daring touches of her hand against his skin, quickly withdrawing in fright whenever she saw the fierce burn of desire darken his eyes.

The day had been hot and still, the fields around the cottage parched brown by the sun; the farmers had been delighted by their early hay crop, and the air was full of dust motes and the scents of summer.

He had been working in the garden. He had taken his reponsibilities towards the owner of the cottage seriously, and she, growing bored and petulant at not receiving his full attention, had mischievously turned the hosepipe full on him, soaking him to the skin.

Even without closing her eyes, she could remember now how the jetting spray of water had plastered the thin cotton of his shirt to his body, darkening his jeans to dense navy. He had stood up slowly and turned towards her. She hadn't been able to remove her gaze from his face. His eyes had burnt as fiercely as a golden hawk's, and she had felt the familiar frisson of sexually generated tension curl through her stomach.

He had advanced on her slowly, stalking her like a soft, padded mountain cat, and she had stood where she was, shaking with excitement and fear. She knew quite well what she had unleashed and she couldn't run from it. When he reached her he would take her in his arms and kiss her until she could hardly breathe for the suffocating sensation of need building inside her . . .

But instead, when he was within feet of her, he picked up the hosepipe and quite deliberately played it over her body, ignoring her shriek of outraged protest.

She was wearing a brief top and shorts. The top was loose and she had seen no need to wear a bra to support the brief uplift of her small breasts, but with the soaking top plastered against her skin and her nipples hardening under the combined shock of the cold water and her own arousal, she suddenly felt as vulnerable as though she were actually naked.

As she crossed her arms protectively over her chest, she heard Silas saying drily, 'Serves you right. You needed cooling off.' But then, when her teeth started to chatter with a mixture of cold and the withdrawal of the momentary high she had been experiencing, his manner changed. He dropped the hosepipe and came towards her, frowning as he observed her stricken face and the tears that were already shimmering in her eyes.

She had still been so much the child . . . so governed by moods that alternated from high to low, Kate recognised wryly. So much a victim of her own emergent sexuality, and so very, very immature . . .

'Hey, come on. It's all right,' he told her softly, prising her arms away from her body, and wrapping her in his own. As an embrace it had been purely comforting, but she was still inclined to sulk, not liking being treated like a child, and she tried to pull away.

The friction caused by the wet cloth against her breasts caused her nipples to harden again, and her angry movements to break free dragged the hardened points against Silas's chest. She had not realised what she was doing until she felt the swelling arousal of his body.

There was a moment when she could have pulled away, when he obviously recognised their danger and momentarily eased back from her, but she pressed wantonly against him, wanting to make him acknowledge the power of her womanhood, and the moment was lost beneath the roaring swell of their mutual desire.

He said her name, thickly, rawly, and she had looked up to see the topaz eyes glittering fires of gold.

He kissed her then, and not just on the mouth,

but all over her body, lying her down on the grass and sucking on her tender, virginal nipples until she writhed in ecstasy, crying out incoherent pleas to have him against her, around her, within her.

He made love to her there under the hot June sun, so that the scent of the garden mingled with the scent of his body, and he loved her in such a way that she found only delight and pride in her body, offering herself up to his most intimate caress without qualm.

They spent the evening lazily loving one another and drinking wine, lying in the huge double bed with its linen sheets and old-fashioned eiderdown.

She spilled some of hers, and it ran down over her breasts and on to her belly.

Her stomach quivered protestingly as she had a vivid memory of Silas's dark head bent over her body. If she closed her eyes, she suspected she might actually feel again the rough sensuality of his tongue as it had lapped at the spilt wine.

And after that . . . She shook as she tried not to remember how the touch of his tongue had aroused her, and how she in turn had stroked and tasted every inch of him.

In the morning she had felt an unfamiliar soreness, and she had been as lazy as a cream-fed cat: too sated to want to move. They had made love again in the hot stillness of the afternoon, Silas deliberately arousing her to a pitch where she had cried out her need and pleasure, and he had responded fiercely to the eroticism of the sounds she had made.

They had been lovers from June to September,

and Silas had told her that they would get married at Christmas. He wanted her to be a winter bride, he had told her, because it would so suit her colouring, and afterwards he would make love to her in the light from an open fire and watch the flames play red-gold against her pale skin while he fulfilled their marital vows. But he had been lying to her . . .

It was the sound of voices around her that brought Kate back to the present. She reached up to make sure that the warmth of her skin was not her own hot tears, that she need not brush them away. She had done all her crying for Silas years ago, and when Cherry was born she had told herself that she was going to put him out of her mind completely.

And she had succeeded.

Until she came back to Abbeydale.

Had he fallen in love with her birthplace? she wondered. Perhaps he planned to breed a flock of the sheep he had shown her; if so, her father would be envious.

But how would she feel with Silas living close at hand? And what about Cherry? So far her daughter had evinced only the most basic curiosity about her father, but as she matured . . .

So many problems. None of which Kate could solve, so to take her mind off them she asked curiously, 'You don't seem to have any females on the staff.'

'No,' one of the men told her with a grin. 'It isn't deliberate, but most of the qualified women in this field have husbands and families, which could lead to complications in this particular instance.'

She could see that, Kate acknowledged, accepting a cup of coffee from Larry and thanking him for her meal. He flushed darkly, reminding her how young he was.

Once, she had been like that, wearing her every emotion on her face.

After dinner, Kate returned to Silas's house and went straight to her own room. She had learned from the others that he frequently worked late into the evening, but even so she had no wish for him to think she was deliberately hanging around, hoping for his company.

At nine o'clock she rang the farm to say goodnight to Cherry. It was just as well that her daughter had taken so well to her grandparents, Kate reflected as she stared out of the window, and wished she could develop more enthusiasm for the new term projects she ought to be working on.

At half-past nine she acknowledged that there was no way she was going to work.

Pulling on a warm sweater, she went outside.

Although they were past Midsummer Day, up here the nights were lighter, tonight particularly so, Kate reflected as she headed towards the park area of the grounds. A walk and some fresh air, both would surely help her sleep.

And yet as she walked, instead of being more peaceful, her thoughts became more turbulent: images of Silas when she had first known him flitting through her mind like silent, reproachful ghosts.

Reproachful? She stopped abruptly, frowning to herself, an elusive awareness she had had ever since he had first looked at her this afternoon suddenly crystallising into realisation. But why should Silas want to reproach her, and for what? Unless their affair had been the cause of the break-up of his marriage and he blamed her for that fact.

Their affair. The very words left an acid taste in her mouth. But how else was she to describe their relationship?

A four-legged shape bounded out of the shadows ahead of her, but the male voice that shouted sharply, 'Max' did not belong to the dog's official handler, and Kate was half inclined to turn and flee as she recognised Silas coming towards her.

Dusk was falling quite rapidly now, and she realised she had been out longer than she had originally intended.

'It's all right. Max and I understand one another,' she told Silas as the dog came up to her and he motioned it back. It sat down at her feet, tail beating on the ground and she rubbed absently behind its ears.

'Yes. You always did have an affinity with them.'

She was surprised that he remembered such a small detail about her, and to cover her confusion said rapidly, 'I think it's something that goes with being a Seton. Cherry is animal-mad. She has already decided she wants to be a vet when she grows up.'

'Cherry?'

She couldn't see him frowning, but she could hear it in his voice.

'My daughter,' she told him stiffly.

'Yes, of course. I'd heard you had a child. How old is she seven . . . eight?'

Kate stared at him. He had no idea at all that Cherry was his; it was so obvious that he had never even given the possibility a thought. Even if she told him Cherry's real age, she thought cynically, it would probably not mean anything to him.

'A little older than that,' she said evasively, and then, determined to put the past behind her completely, she asked in a determinedly bright voice, 'And your two boys, how old are they now?'

They had started to walk back towards the house, Max padding silently at their heels. Once they had shared many long walks, and they seemed to fall into step automatically, but now Silas stopped abruptly, and as he turned towards her the twilight illuminated his features, giving them an odd starkness.

'My what?' he demanded.

Surely, after all this time, he wasn't going to keep up the pretence? What would be the point? It angered Kate that he couldn't be open and honest with her, and she deliberately did not allow herself to reflect that she had not been totally honest with him in allowing him to think that Cherry was another man's child.

'You know what I'm talking about, Silas, so don't pretend you don't,' she snapped angrily.

'You may have lost your wife, but . . .'

'What wife? I have no wife,' he interrupted her flatly.

'Don't lie to me. I may have been idiotic enough to fall for it once, but not now. I saw you with her, Silas. I heard you talking to her. I heard her saying how much the boys had missed you. I saw you kissing her . . .'

The silence seemed to go on for ever, the tension it bred leaving Kate shaky and sick. Just merely talking about seeing him with his wife had brought back the scene so vividly that she could actually feel the same disbelief and despair she had experienced then, the same horrified realisation that Silas had lied to her, the same knowledge that what she had overheard had changed her world for ever.

As she had done then, she placed her hands over her still flat stomach.

The thought that she might be pregnant was something that had only just begun to occur to her. Her period was a few days late, that was all, but already she was beginning to worry. After that first time they had made love, Silas had cautioned her that they must not take any further risks, and she had told him that she would make arrangements to ensure that she was fully protected. Only she hadn't done so; the time she spent either with Silas or daydreaming about him had meant that she was falling behind with her studies, and with the careless insouciance of youth she had put the matter to the back of her mind.

Until that week. Then the thought that she

might actually be carrying Silas's child made her feel both proud and nervous. They had talked about having a family, but they both had studies to finish and, although she had assured him that she wanted to be married as quickly as they could arrange it, Silas had insisted that she must finish her studies first. She might not mind now, but later . . .

She had pouted and sulked a little, and then remembering his cautionary words, she had been apprehensive about telling him of her fears.

She had known she would never tell him, and she had stood shivering in the bright sunshine, her youth and happiness destroyed in the space of time it had taken her to witness Silas and the other woman embrace.

Giving herself a tiny shake, Kate dragged her thoughts back to the present.

'Susie isn't my wife,' Silas told her flatly. 'She's my sister.'

He had never talked to her about his family, other than to say that his parents were dead. He had made the announcement in a flat, hard voice that had warned her not to question him.

'I didn't know you had a sister,' she told him in a low, pain-filled voice.

As he registered her confusion, he said quietly, 'Susie's husband and our parents were killed in a motorway pile-up. Simon had gone to collect them so that they could all spend a bank holiday weekend together. They were killed on their way there.

'I'd just started at Lancaster at the time, and I

was torn between giving up the course and finding a job somewhere close to Susie and the boys, or persuading her to bring the boys and come and live with me, but I underestimated her bravery. She insisted on staying in the home she and Simon had built together; she felt the loss of their father and grandparents was enough for the boys to cope with, without inflicting a change of house on them, no matter how painful it was for her to stay there.

'That weekend, she'd come up to tell me that she was remarrying, an old friend of both hers and Simon's.

'I'd known she was coming up, but not why. I'd been selfishly concerned that she might have changed her mind and decided to take up my original offer for her to make a home for herself and the boys with me. I hadn't met you when I'd first suggested it.'

There was just enough light left for her to see the bleakness in his face. Her heart was thudding painfully, the full realisation of what his words actually meant mercifully still not fully dawning on her.

'When she told me she was remarrying, the first thing I wanted to do was to tell you. I told her all about you . . . I'd planned for the three of us to go out for dinner to celebrate, only I couldn't find you.'

She'd taken a bus into Cumbria, Kate remembered, and she'd spent what was left of the day walking until her body ached with fatigue. Even then she hadn't wanted to stop, as though in some way the ceaseless motion was keeping her pain at bay.

She'd spent the night with a couple who did bed and breakfasts, and had left early the next morning, despite their protests that she hadn't had anything to eat.

She'd spent almost a week like that: simply walking, sleeping, eating when her tormented nervous system would let her. And then she'd sent Silas a letter, telling him that she had changed her mind about marrying him and enclosing the small solitaire ring he had bought her.

No period and three consecutive days' worth of early-morning sickness had confirmed her fears that she was pregnant and, having no other option left open to her, she had gone home to tell her parents.

'Was it because you saw me with Susie that you broke our engagement?' Silas asked her in a low voice.

She could hear the shocked disbelief in his voice, and just for a moment she hesitated, but her innate honesty made her tell him the truth.

'Yes.'

'You saw me kiss her, heard us talk about the children, and from that drew the conclusions that I was married with a family? You actually thought that, after everything we'd been to one another?'

'I was eighteen, Silas,' she told him wearily, turning her head so that she wouldn't have to face the accusation in his eyes.

Hearing him put her assumptions into words made them sound so idiotic.

'Why on earth didn't you say something?' he demanded roughly. 'Why just disappear?'

Because I was pregnant . . . because I loved you . . . because I was frightened . . . because I felt hurt and betrayed . . . because I was eighteen and still very much a child.

What could she tell him?

'You're lying to me,' he said roughly. 'Seeing me with Susie was just an excuse.'

Kate shook her head.

'No. I loved you, Silas, but you have to understand . . . I'd had a very narrow upbringing; the very thought of being involved with a man who I thought was committed to someone else went against everything I'd been brought up to believe in. I was confused, jealous, frightened, and so I ran away.'

And you didn't even bother to try and find me, she thought inwardly, so whatever the cause of their break-up had been, whatever his initial shock, there must have come a time when he had decided that it was for the best. And from the vantage point of her own maturity, she herself sincerely doubted if their relationship could have lasted. Those eight years between them had been a vast gulf: she still really a child, unsure of herself, bemused and bedazzled by the thought of him loving her, not really believing it.

She had loved him, but she had not wholly

believed he had loved her, that he *could* love her. The insecurity bred in her by her upbringing, when she had always believed herself inferior to David, second-best to her brother in her parents' affections, had made her feel unsure with Silas, and it was that insecurity which had prompted her to leap to the conclusion that he was committed to someone else, almost as though there was an odd sort of relief in discovering that she had been right not to believe that he could love her.

'I don't think I believe this. God, I don't know if I *want* to believe it,' she heard Silas groan, and in the half-darkness she saw him shake his head and then reach out as though he intended to touch her.

Instinctively she stepped back, and saw the shutters come down over his eyes, his expression hardening as he, too, stepped back.

'Well, it's all one hell of a long time ago, and scarcely important now,' he said curtly. 'When did you get married?' he added carelessly.

He had started to move off in the direction of the house, and she had automatically followed him. Now she stopped, almost missing her step.

'I'm not married,' she told him indistinctly, watching him swing round and stare frowningly at her. 'I never have been married,' she elucidated proudly, her chin tilting, her eyes defying him to comment.

There was a brief hiatus, and then he asked evenly, 'And the man who fathered your child, are you and he still together? Or did you dump him, too?'

His words were bitterly unfair, and angry tears burned at the back of her eyes.

'Cherry's father isn't part of our lives,' she told him, adding fiercely, 'and we don't need him to be.'

'You mean, *you* don't need him to be,' he retaliated. 'Your daughter . . . his daughter . . . might have different views.'

'If you're trying to suggest that Cherry is in any way deprived . . .'

'I'm not suggesting anything,' he told her tiredly. 'I was just wondering what you told him when you dumped him. Or was he the one to do the walking away this time? Fatherhood and responsibility don't suit every man. One of the reasons I got this appointment was because I was single and unencumbered. It came as quite a shock when I realised that the new research centre was going to be here, but a few discreet enquiries soon informed me that John Seton's daughter never came home and that there was a rift between her and her family. Didn't they approve of the way you lived, Kate? It must have been hard for a man like your father to accept that his grandchild was illegitimate.'

They were at the house now, and Silas unlocked the door, standing back to let her in first.

'Aren't you coming in?' she asked him when he turned to walk away.

'I've got some stuff in the computer I want to check.'

'But, Silas, you worked right through dinner! You look exhausted.' She saw him flinch slightly and bit down hard on her bottom lip, cursing her lack of tact.

'It's too late to start playing the concerned little woman now, Kate,' he told her harshly.

And as he walked away she heard him add beneath his breath, 'Eleven damn years too late.'

CHAPTER SIX

KATE couldn't go to bed; she was more wide awake now than she had been before, every nerve-end jumping, her mind a jumble of discordant facts. She paced the kitchen restlessly, and then made herself a cup of coffee.

Nursing the hot mug, she sat down, staring into space. Silas not married, not a father . . . And he never had been.

Oh, God, what had she done? She thought of Cherry, of her bright intelligence and her warm, loving personality, and she thought of the relationship she should have had with Silas and guilty tears stung her eyes again.

She was the one who was responsible for depriving Cherry of her father. *She* was the one, not Silas. And all because she had been too immature, too insecure to ask one simple question. How on earth was she going to live with the knowledge?

She was still trying to find an answer for herself hours later when she fell asleep. And Silas had still not come in.

It was pointless wishing she could turn the clock back. By the very fact that he had made no attempt to find her, Silas had shown how indifferent he had been to their broken engagement.

The pain, the anguish, the bitterness she had

seen briefly in his eyes—those must spring from another source rather than her own defection. And yet, when he had looked at her as she had accused him of being married, there had been a look in his eyes that had made her want to cross the gap between them, take him in her arms and tell him that whatever his pain she would make it go away.

So much for the value of experience and maturity. At heart, she wasn't so very different from the girl she had been at eighteen. Then, she had looked at Silas and ached to have him as her lover, to be loved by him; and now, at twenty-nine, going on thirty, she had looked at him tonight and known that if he reached out to her, if he touched her, she wouldn't be able to stop herself from begging him to take her in his arms, to forgive her for her stupidity. To . . .

To what? Say they could start again? Life wasn't like that. They had a child, and she had allowed Silas to believe that Cherry had been fathered by someone else.

What else could she have done? Baldly announce that Cherry was his? What if he had refused to believe her, accused her of lying? Or worse, what if he had still remained totally indifferent? Or what if he had demanded parental rights to Cherry? What if he had said that he wanted to know the daughter she had denied him? How would she have been able to cope with that? No, it was better that he didn't know.

This present situation wouldn't last. In a week's time, they would part and go their separate ways, and probably never meet again.

She found the thought less than comforting.

In the morning there was still no sign of Silas. His bedroom door was open, his bed unslept in.

Downstairs, Kate ate a solitary breakfast and then rang the farm.

Cherry sounded slightly subdued, and Kate had to work hard at enforcing a bright note of cheerfulness into her own voice, but by the time she had hung up Cherry was her normal bright, bubbly self.

After breakfast, time hung heavily on her hands; she felt honour-bound not to cause any more problems than she already had, which meant keeping away from the main building, and eating solitary lunch with less and less enthusiasm.

The whole day went by without her seeing a soul.

Her only contact with other human beings was her telephone calls home. Max appeared several times, simply scratching at the back door, and greeting her with very obvious pleasure when she let him in.

Her interest in the new term's curriculum palled in the afternoon. She explored every inch of the home park. The evening dragged, Silas remained absent and she went to bed early—feeling irritable and lonely. To wake up the next day and find the sky heavy with rain-clouds was the last straw.

On impulse, she pulled on wellingtons and a weatherproof coat and set off for the main building.

Just as she reachd it, Graham emerged.

'Hello,' he greeted her. 'Anything I can do to help?'

'Not unless you can find me something to do,' Kate told him ruefully.

'Easily,' he responded quickly. 'Especially if you happen to have some computer experience.'

Kate did, having taken several intensive courses on various aspects of the new computer technology, and what Graham wanted her to do was simply to monitor several very basic programmes, leaving him free to write up some reports.

'We'd better not let Silas know we've got a computer expert here,' he joked with Andy Lewis, one of the vets in charge of the experimental unit. 'Otherwise we're going to lose her.'

Graham's office was a cluttered, busy place and, recognising that he was one of that breed of people who worked best from an untidy mind, Kate wasn't surprised that he was having problems adjusting to the new technology. He admitted quite frankly to her that he preferred more old-fashioned methods, and was full of praise at the speed with which Kate dealt with the backlog of work.

As far as she was concerned, it was a relief to have something to do, and she was just telling him so when the door opened and Silas walked in.

He checked when he saw her, an unguarded look of anguished uncertainty crossing his face, and then he took a step towards her, stopping abruptly.

'Graham, I've run out of pain-killers, do you

have any?' he requested the doctor, turning his back on Kate.

'I have, but you know that I've warned you about these attacks of yours, Silas. You drive yourself far too hard. The world won't collapse if you stop working twenty-four hours a day, you know.'

'Maybe not,' Silas agreed grimly. 'But the government might withdraw our funding. You know very well that we're on a time limit here to produce results, Graham, and you know how I feel about the importance of checking every piece of research. Powerful drugs produce powerful side-effects.'

'Here are your tablets,' Graham told him, unlocking a medical cabinet and extracting a small bottle. 'I hope I don't have to tell you that if you intend to take these you've got to go home and go straight to bed.'

'I may be a fool,' Silas told him drily, 'but I'm not that much of one.'

He turned to go, still having not even acknowledged Kate's presence other than by that brief startled look when he had walked in. She could see that he was in pain now; his eyes were darkly glazed with it, and his skin was sweating slightly.

'Kate's proved a godsend,' Graham told him cheerfully as he walked with him to the door. 'She's even been able to master the intricacies of that infernal computer you've cursed me with.'

Silas did look at her then, checking and frowning, 'Kate's been working in here?'

The accusatory note in his voice angered her. Her chin tilted proudly, her eyes darkening with emotion.

'It's all right, Silas,' she told him disdainfully. 'I'm perfectly well aware of the confidential nature of the work being done here. You may not believe it, but as a teacher, I am used to dealing with confidential information and . . .'

'I asked her if she could help out, Silas,' Graham intervened placatingly. 'The records are beginning to get in one hell of a mess. You know yourself, you said only the other day that we could do with some professional clerical assistance.'

'Yes, I know,' Silas agreed. 'And you know how the Ministry feels about our taking on extra staff. Dammit, Graham, they're already looking for a reason to close us down, and if it wasn't for the success we had in Ethiopia, we wouldn't even have got this far . . .'

'I know, and I know how much this research means to you, Silas.'

'A strain of sheep that can live and breed in any climate, provide meat and high quality wool, and that can live off virtually the poorest grass . . .'

'Yes, it's a very ambitious project,' Graham agreed. 'And another few more months of tests to prove that these animals are virtually disease-immune and you'll have everything you need to convince the authorities to go ahead and approve the new strain.'

'I thought you were trying to find an antidote for rabies,' Kate interrupted them. She had assumed that the development of the new strain of sheep was simply a side issue, but from their conversation it appeared that she was wrong.

'That was just gossip started when we first came here,' Silas told her abruptly. 'It helped to keep people away, which was what we wanted, and so we didn't deny it.'

'But the security . . . the quarantine . . .'

'Our sheep have deliberately been infected with several of the most virulent sheep diseases there are. If only one of those animals gets out, it could infect every flock for miles around and totally decimate them.

'Another week and we'll know for sure that our animals are disease-free. Hence the quarantine. We can't afford to take any risks. Not even the slight risk that you could possibly indirectly cause an outbreak of disease among the fell flocks.'

'That would have been a very remote chance,' Kate challenged him hotly. 'If you'd only told me that, I'd . . .'

'You'd have what? Refused to accept my quarantine ruling?' Silas snapped at her. 'I meant every word I said, Kate. You're staying.'

And with that he turned and opened the door.

Kate watched him, and then realised that Graham was watching her rather curiously. A painful flush stained her skin as she realised he had overheard that familiar 'Kate' that had sat so easily on Silas's lips. The way he had said her name had not spoken of a recent or unfamiliar relationship.

'Will he be all right on his own?' she asked awkwardly, trying to bridge the difficult moment.

'I should think so. He's had enough practice. Of course, if you're concerned, you could always go back with him.'

'What's wrong with him exactly?' Kate asked, avoiding a direct answer.

'He contracted a severe and debilitating attack of . . . fever . . . whilst he was working in Ethiopia with the famine relief organisations. Every now and again the fever recurs. It shouldn't, and if he didn't push himself so hard it wouldn't. In its own way it's at least fifty per cent pyschosomatic—his body's way of telling him that it's had enough. Known him long, have you?' he added casually.

Kate stiffened.

'I was with him out there,' Graham told her quietly. 'During the worst of his fever he became delirious. I've often wondered who Kate was and what happened to her. He fought like a caged tiger to persuade the government to give us a different venue for this research station, but in the end he had no alternative. It was this place or nothing.'

There was absolutely nothing Kate could say.

Silas alone, sick, crying out for her . . . It was as though someone had plunged a knife into her stomach and was cruelly turning it.

Kate put off returning to the house for as long as she could. Not because she was frightened of seeing Silas, but because she was terrified of what her own reaction might be.

She had known the moment she had seen him that, physically, he still affected her. Mature now, she had found it all too easy to recognise that pulsing excitement of her flesh, even though it was a sensation she had not experienced in all the long years without him.

And now, like the advent calendars Cherry so loved at Christmas, slowly and tantalisingly small pieces of a Silas she had not really known existed were being revealed to her. And, as an adult, her perceptions honed by her years of experience, it was as though she was seeing the whole man for the first time, and not just the Silas she had adored as her lover.

That man had existed for her in one dimension only, that dimension being his relationship with her. Oh, they had talked of their future together, but she had always seen that future bathed in the rosy light of perfection of them together, married, with children; although she supposed she must have known of Silas's great need to improve the lot of humanity, she had selfishly pushed it to one side as something of far less importance than her own feelings.

She stopped abruptly as she walked down the lane, tears stinging her eyes. She rubbed them away grimly. Tears for Silas, or for herself?

The first thing she heard when she walked into the house was the sound of a typewriter. Without thinking, she opened the door to Silas's study and stood there.

He was dressed only in pyjama bottoms, his feet bare, his hair tousled, his forehead pleated in a frown of concentration.

'I thought Graham said you weren't to work,' she reminded him tartly.

Just for a moment he looked surprised, a glimmer of something that could have been amusement lighting his eyes and making her flush as she realised how bossy she probably sounded.

But he made no comment other than to say pointedly, 'I wasn't until the telephone rang. Your daughter sounds very like you.'

Her daughter. He had spoken to Cherry . . . She felt panic hit her. He was saying something to her; she forced herself to concentrate on it. Something about children.

'You always wanted a family, didn't you? I remember you saying you wanted at least four children.'

Had she said that? She couldn't remember. Cherry was their child and she loved her, but her experience as a teacher had soon destroyed her illusions, and she was well aware now that the relationship between parent and child was not always so harmonious as the one she had with Cherry.

'What happened to the other three?' he taunted her unkindly.

Kate stared at him, and then gathered her wits to say waspishly, 'At least I have a child. You haven't even achieved that much.'

It was a lie, but he was hardly likely to know it, nor to care; and yet, as she focused on him, she saw him go white to the bone, as though she had dealt him a mortal blow. He removed his hands from the keyboard of the machine, but not before she had seen their convulsive jerk, as though something she had said had hit a raw nerve.

It had been stupid to retaliate so childishly to his taunt. More worthy of the eighteen-year-old she had been than the woman she was. He must think her as immature now as she had been then. And she suddenly realised she wanted him to have a good opinion of her.

'I'm sorry, that was an idiotic thing to say,' she apologised quietly. 'But I am surprised that you haven't married and had a family, Silas. You were always so marvellous with children. Remember that little girl on the fell . . .'

'If I ever wanted children, then I certainly don't want them now,' he told her harshly. 'There isn't room in my life for that kind of commitment any more.'

Kate stared at him, wondering at the suppressed passion in his voice and the bitterness in his eyes. He had changed so much; she barely recognised him, and not just because her own perception of him had changed, she acknowledged. The Silas she had known had wanted a family, had loved children; that hadn't been a figment of her infatuated imaginings. She remembered how she had fatuously agreed with him, promising him that their first child would be a son, only to be told that he would prefer a daughter.

Ironic, the twists fate took.

'You didn't have any lunch,' she said quietly. 'When I've phoned Cherry, I could make some supper.'

'No, thanks,' he told her curtly. 'I'm going back to bed.'

As he stood up, she quickly averted her gaze

from the sight of his half-clothed body.

Had she really once had the freedom to reach out and touch that solid expanse of flesh and sinew? The tingling in her fingertips told her that she had, that her fevered memories of the sensation of that dark coating of fine, silky hair beneath them was no mere imagining.

Her mouth went dry suddenly, as she recalled how she had once covered him with adoring kisses. She couldn't drag her attention away from the dark, hard nubs of flesh she had once teased with her mouth and, appallingly, her own nipples suddenly hardened and pulsed with arousal.

She was shaking as she finally managed to look away, and then she saw it: a fine criss-cross of white scars low down on the left-hand side of his body.

Unable to stop herself, she gave a low cry and reached out to touch him with fingers that trembled.

'What happened?' she asked huskily, unable to stop focusing on the scarred flesh. Her fingertips quivered sensitively over the ridged flesh. Tears gushing hotly into her eyes, she wanted to take him into her arms the way she did Cherry when she was hurt, and to press her lips to his skin in a gesture of solace and anguish.

'A tribesman's knife,' she heard Silas saying tautly above her. 'An accident. It became inflamed and wouldn't heal.'

He didn't tell her about the lack of antibiotics, about the lack of anything but the most primitive medical facilities; and how even then he had been racked with guilt for taking medication desperately needed to help people who were dying in their thousands.

He looked down at her and ached to reach out and touch her. It all seemed so long ago now. He had gone out to Ethiopia on impulse after she had broken their engagement. An impetuous decision which had brought home to him in a very real sense man's inhumanity to his own kind.

There was so much compassion and emotion within her. The woman she had matured into was so much more than the girl had been. She took his breath away, seized his emotions, made him want to cry out to the heavens to roll back the years.

He had loved her then and he loved her now, but she had left him and another man had given her a child.

Her head moved. In another second he would feel her mouth against his skin.

He shivered violently and pushed her away.

Kate came abruptly to her senses, flushing with mortification as she stepped back from him.

'I must go and ring Cherry,' she said awkwardly, and fled to her room where she sat on her bed, a tight bundle of tensed arms and legs, berating herself for her idiocy.

All right, so he wasn't married, never had been married, but that didn't mean that she could simply walk back into his life and expect him to welcome her with open arms.

Walk back into his life. Was that what she wanted?

Yes . . . *Yes*. She wanted to take him and show

him their daughter, to tell him that she had never stopped loving him. But he thought Cherry was another man's child, she remembered abruptly. He had also told her that there was no room in his life for a wife and child.

Had he been warning her off then? Had he recognised what was happening to her before she realised it herself? Had that been his way of telling her there was no going back, that there was no longer any place for her in his life?

Sadly, she recognised that, for Cherry's sake, there was no way she could reveal the truth and risk her daughter perhaps being rejected by the man who had fathered her. Proud though she was of the child they had created together, for Cherry's sake she must allow Silas to go on believing that there had been someone else in her life and that that someone else was Cherry's father.

Silas left the study and walked slowly to the stairs. He had been a fool to pretend to himself that he could have her living in the same house with him without it affecting him. It had been the discovery that she had thought he was married that had thrown him off guard.

All these years he had thought that she had simply panicked and left him because she had felt trapped, because she had been too young to commit herself to marriage—something which even at the time he had known, but which he in his need had dismissed.

He had never been able to blame her for breaking their engagement, rather blaming himself for taking advantage of her youth; and now, the discovery that she had not left him for the reason he had thought had totally thrown him.

But her life had gone on, as had his own, with one important difference. She had obviously found someone else to love, a someone else by whom she had had a child. As he walked upstairs, he found he was sweating, and yet he felt icy-cold at the same time. A child. He started to shiver. She had always wanted children . . . they both had—then.

He was shivering violently by the time he reached his bedroom. He crawled into the untidy bed and huddled down under the bedclothes, closing his eyes, but despite the medication he had taken sleep would not come.

Instead, he was tormented by memories of the past. Of Kate, as she had been when he first knew her. His memories unravelled mockingly. Kate, so shy and inexperienced, so loving and giving, and yet at the same time so unsure of herself, not knowing how she tormented him with her innocent sexuality. And then later, when they were lovers. He made an anguished sound of despair and rolled over on to his stomach.

Who was the man by whom she had had her child? Where was he? It was obvious that he was no longer part of her life. Had she loved him? Stupid question; knowing Kate, she must have done. She obviously loved his child.

Again the pain struck, and he cried out with it.

In her room, Kate heard him, and tensed as though his pain were her own. She wanted to go to him, and yet she felt she could not. The way he had pushed her away when she had tried to touch his scar had shown her that.

She picked up the telephone and dialled the number of the farm. Her father answered, and beneath the familiar gruffness of his voice she sensed his love and concern.

'How's Cherry?' she asked him huskily.

'Missing you,' he told her. 'But that's only natural. The two of you've never been apart before, so she tells us. You've done a fine job of bringing her up, lass.' She heard him draw a deep breath, and then he added roughly, 'Don't worry about her. We'll see she's all right.'

There were tears in Kate's eyes when she spoke to Cherry, and she recognised guiltily that for those few minutes while she had been with Silas, when she had reached out to touch him, she had almost forgotten that their child even existed. That was the intensity of the effect he had on her. From the moment she was born, Cherry had been the focus of her life. She swallowed hard and tried to answer Cherry's questions about her day as honestly as she could.

'What's he like, the man who runs the station?' Cherry asked her curiously.

It was a natural enough question, and yet Kate froze. When she eventually replaced the receiver she was shaking with fear.

She knew she ought to have something to eat, but the thought of food nauseated her.

Outside it was still light, too early to go to bed. Besides, she wasn't tired. In fact, she was far too keyed-up. It was a sensation she remembered vividly from her early days of knowing Silas, only now it came without the heady excitement she had known then: the tense excitement that all girls on the brink of love experience. Now there was just that tense, thrilling fear; that sense of sickening certainty that she loved a man without any hope of ever having her love returned.

She shivered and walked into the study where Silas had been working. What was it about him that made her feel like this? He was only a man, like any other; she was an attractive woman who had attracted her share of male interest over the years, but none of the other men she had met had ever made her feel like this.

His desk was untidy with papers; some of them had slipped on to the floor. She bent to pick them up, and as she did so she caught her arm painfully on the corner of an open drawer. Rubbing the tender place, she tried to shut the drawer, but something was jammed inside it.

Feeling carefully inside, she managed to dislodge the photograph frame that had been caught up against the back of the drawer.

She hadn't meant to pry, but she had to remove it from the drawer to make it close, and her heart turned over as she saw her own eighteen-year-old reflection staring back at her through the glass.

All these years he had kept her photograph. The image blurred and trembled as tears burned her eyes. Kneeling on the floor beside the desk, she let them fall. She had once vowed she had wept enough tears for Silas and that she would weep no more.

But those tears hadn't been for Silas, they had been selfish tears for herself, *these* were for Silas, and all that her teenage idiocy had cost them both.

How soon after she had left him had he gone to Ethiopia? Very carefully and slowly she put the photograph back. Then she got up slowly, without disturbing his papers.

It wouldn't do for him to guess that she had found it.

It was late when she went to bed. She had deliberately dawdled, half hoping that Silas would wake up and come downstairs, and that they would talk as they had once done, with so much to say to one another that the hours flew by on silver wings. But of course he hadn't done so, and even if they had . . . What was there for them to talk about now?

As a mother, Kate had learned long ago to sleep lightly, and so when she heard the sharp, anguished cry she was out of bed and by her bedroom door before she was even properly awake; instincts honed over the years of caring for Cherry carrying her to Silas's bedside almost in her sleep.

It wasn't until he cried out again that she realised what he had said, her whole body turning cold as he repeated her name in a raw, tormented voice of need.

He had thrown off the bedclothes, and the silver light from outside revealed a faint sheen of sweat on his skin.

As she bent over him, one hand smoothing back the dark tangle of his hair, the other instinctively measuring the heat coming off his skin and trying to gauge the degree of his fever, he opened his eyes.

'Kate,' he said wonderingly, 'you're here.'

And he looked at her with such a shining look of gratitude that she could hardly speak for the lump in her throat.

Did he realise what he was saying? Where he was? Was he remembering their conversation earlier, or in his fever had he slipped back to a time where the pain of reality couldn't touch him?

'Stay with me,' he begged her huskily, his fingers curling round her wrist and holding on to her. 'Stay with me, Kate . . .'

She shuddered as desire swept through her like sheet-lightning.

This was crazy; she couldn't stay with him. She shouldn't even be contemplating it. He didn't even realise what he was saying. She went to prise his grip off her arm, but, as she bent her head to do so, he lifted his own. His eyes were bright with fever, his skin fire-hot.

'Oh, God, Kate, you don't know how much I've missed you,' he told her rawly, and then he dropped his head on to her shoulder, burying his face in her hair, and she heard him saying indistinctly, 'Hold me, Kate. Please hold me.'

And, as he released her wrist and raised his head to look at her, she opened her arms to him, and felt her body tremble with delight at the familiar warmth and weight of him, so well remembered despite all the years without him.

CHAPTER SEVEN

KATE woke up first. At some stage during the night, she must have got into bed with Silas, and now he was lying with his head against her chest, his breath just moving the lace that trimmed her nightgown.

As she tried to ease herself away, he opened his eyes.

'So you weren't just a dream,' he said quietly.

Kate had never felt more uncomfortable in her life. He had the excuse of being gripped by a fever which had rendered him virtually incapable of knowing either what he was saying or what he was doing. She had no such excuse.

'I . . . I didn't mean to stay,' she gulped nervously, and to her chagrin her throat clogged with tears.

'I'm glad you did,' Silas told her softly, and then, easing himself slightly away from her, he lifted one of her hands to his mouth and pressed a kiss into her palm.

Her skin tingled, vibrating with a thousand dangerous sensations. His face was rough with overnight beard, his lips hard and warm. She felt his tongue touch the pads of her fingertips, and she shuddered in reaction, her breath escaping on a hurried gasp.

'Gentle, compassionate Kate.' He looked at her

wryly. 'I hope I didn't make too much of a fool of myself.'

'No. You . . . I . . .'

She was breathing far too fast, desperate suddenly to put a safe distance between them. It had seemed quite reasonable last night to take a feverish, vulnerable Silas into her arms and to hold him as she had so often held their daughter, but this Silas, who was looking at her with clear gold eyes, who was still holding her hand and measuring the rapid thud of her pulse with his thumb, must surely be aware of exactly what was happening to her. He could hardly fail to be aware of it, she acknowledged blushingly, knowing without having to look down at her body that, where the fabric of her nightgown was flattened against her breasts, the taut arousal of her nipples was clearly visible.

He had seen it, she recognised, her breath catching in her lungs as his gaze dipped to her breasts and stayed there.

'Beautiful Kate,' he said softly, and then his hand cupped the soft weight of her breast and his thumb traced the hard outline of its peak. Her breath became locked in her lungs and she was trembling with a mixture of arousal and embarrassment.

'Silas, please,' she began, but he wasn't listening to her.

His weight pressed her down into the bed, his hand cupping her breast possessively, his mouth a mere breath away from her own, as he breathed roughly, 'Kate, it's been so long. Too long.'

And then he was kissing her. Not as she remembered him kissing her, but as a man kisses a woman who has been greatly desired and greatly longed for, easing her mouth under his own and keeping it there while he fed ravenously on the sweetness of it.

His hands left her body to thread into her hair and hold her head still on the pillow while he kissed her and then kissed her again, parting the trembling bow of her mouth so that he could taste her more intimately.

In the past, when they had made love, she had taken the pleasure that Silas had so generously given her with all the hedonistic selfishness of the very young.

This time it was different. This time she was a woman. This time her pleasure in knowing him was tinged already with pain, with knowing that at best this could be only the most fleeting of moments, that her responsibility was to Cherry and that she was no longer free to consider only herself. Silas had made it plain that a wife and children were encumbrances he did not want, and so, in the knowledge that there could only be this private brief intimacy, Kate allowed her love for him to sweep away all her inhibitions and reservations.

When the time came to pay the price for this time with Silas, she would be ready for it, and no matter what that price was nothing would make her regret what she was now sharing with him, she told herself fiercely as she slid her palms over his shoulders, rediscovering the strong column of his neck, the thick silkiness of his hair as she cupped the back of his head and opened her mouth to the insistent thrust of his tongue.

The first time he had kissed her like this she had been shocked and then thrilled, but now she was mature in body and mind and she responded gladly to his hunger, mentally giving up thanks that he should reveal it to her. She knew how much he wanted her, could feel it in the aroused weight of his body against her own, and yet he did not rush her. And, remembering how he had gently coaxed her through those first few times they had made love, she could have cried for the cruelness of fate in decreeing that their lives should lie apart.

How could he be so compassionate and considerate as a lover, and yet so cold and hard as a man? Or was it simply that his career meant so much to him that he would allow nothing to come before it?

Not a wife, not a child . . . not anything.

'Kate.'

She shuddered as the sound of her name on his tongue became lost against her breast, and then shuddered again, letting her mind slide into hot, velvet darkness as he slid her body free of her nightgown.

It was she who caught hold of him and pulled him down to her, seeing his shuddering recognition of his body's need of her as he cupped the weight of her breast and said huskily, 'You're different. Here . . .'

He opened his mouth over her breast and

caressed it gently. 'And here . . .'

His hand shaped her waist, his breath a tantalising caress against her breast's aching peak, but she wasn't eighteen any more, and she hid the urgency of her need in order to torment him a little in punishment for his own torment of her, running her palm lazily along his body to his hipbone, and then touching the old scar tissue with stroking fingertips as she murmured, 'So are you. Here,' she kissed the point of his shoulder, 'so much broader now, surely, and here, too, I think . . .' Her fingertips fluttered against the arch of his lower ribs, and she felt the unsteady, urgent breath he released.

'And, of course, here too.'

She touched the scar again and felt him flinch slightly. She looked at him and saw the film of perspiration dampen his skin, and the look in his eyes before he veiled it from her, and her own heartbeat picked up the rapid pace of his.

She had seen clearly in his eyes how much he wanted her to touch him, and as she slid the soft heat of her mouth along his body he cried out to her hoarsely and then moaned a raw denial as her lips touched the scarred flesh. She felt his body shudder and flinch beneath her mouth, his fingers digging into her shoulder, but he didn't push her away.

She wanted to love him as completely and generously as he had once loved her; she wanted to show him that now she was adult, able to give pleasure as well as to take it.

Yet as soon as she tried to touch him intimately

he cried out and caught hold of her, protesting harshly, 'No, Kate. Don't.'

But, when she ignored him and her mouth touched the flesh of his inner thigh, he released her, his body jerking spasmodically as he fought to control its response to her, his voice thick and raw with all that he was trying to conceal as he protested, 'Kate, No . . .' And then, 'Oh, God, Kate. *Kate . . .*'

But she wasn't allowed to give him that final pleasure, because he caught hold of her and rolled her beneath him, pinning her there with his weight, caressing every inch of her skin with hands that trembled.

And then his mouth followed the path of his hands, until she cried out to him as he had done to her, and then he buried himself within her, carrying them both quickly to a climax that made her realise how very pale a shadow of reality her memories actually were.

Complete and content, Kate lay in the protection of his arm and looked at him.

His eyes were closed, faint sunken shadows around them marking the toll of his fever. As though he felt her gaze, he opened them and said quietly, 'Forgive me . . . but it's been a long time.'

Something shadowed and painful darkened his eyes; a memory that Kate felt jealously took him away from her. She knew he was thinking of the last woman to whom he had made love, and she wanted to demand to know who she was, but she knew she didn't have the right.

Instead she said softly, 'For me as well . . .'

Instantly, he frowned.

'Was I too rough? Did I hurt you? You should have said.'

'You didn't hurt me.'

They looked at one another for a long time, and she wondered if he was remembering, as she was, the first time they had made love and he had asked her that same question. Then she had pouted a little before giving him her response. She sighed over how young she had been.

'There's no one else in your life, then?'

His hand found hers, so much larger and harder, his fingers twining gently with her own.

'No one,' she told him gravely, her stomach quivering slightly as he raised her hand to his mouth and slowly kissed each finger.

'And the man who fathered your child. Do you love him?' Her face gave her away and she heard him sigh faintly as he said, 'Yes, of course you do. I shouldn't have asked the question. I won't ask you why you're not with him.'

He said it cynically, and Kate felt her skin start to overheat. What was he thinking? That Cherry was the result of some kind of underhand liaison with a man who wasn't in a position to marry her?

'He isn't a married man, if that's what you're thinking,' she told him heatedly.

'But he isn't free to provide a home for you and his child,' Silas persisted.

'He doesn't want to,' Kate told him shortly. Suddenly she felt very cold and alone. 'He's like you, Silas,' she told him harshly. 'He doesn't want the encumbrances of a wife and family.'

She ached for him to deny it, to tell her that he hadn't married in all these years because he still loved her. She ached for him to give her an opportunity to tell him the truth, safe in the knowledge that he would want to know that Cherry was his child, but instead he turned away from her. A tiny muscle flickered sporadically in his jaw, a sure sign that he was tense and angry.

She had known that she would have to pay for the pleasure of those moments of intimacy with him, but she had not known she would be called upon to pay so soon.

'I'd better go back to my own room,' she told him briefly.

'Kate . . .'

'Don't say anything, Silas. What's the point? Let's just both accept what happened and leave it at that, shall we?'

'If that's what you want.'

What she *wanted* . . . What she wanted was for him to take her back in his arms and tell her he was never going to let her go, she admitted as she turned away from him, her eyes stinging with tears she dared not shed.

How on earth was she going to endure the rest of this period of enforced intimacy with him?

Back in her own bed, she watched the dawn creep across the sky. A new day, but she took no pleasure in the thought. For her, all the remaining days of her life would be haunted by Silas and her love for him.

Ridiculously, after what had happened, she overslept, and it was Silas coming into her room who woke her.

To her consternation she saw that he was fully dressed and, worse, that he was carrying a cup of tea.

'Feeling OK?' he asked her softly, putting it down beside the bed.

Pain hit her, swamping her. He could be so tender, so caring; it was hard to accept that he didn't love her and didn't want their child.

'Of course I am,' she replied irritably. 'For heaven's sake, Silas, last night wasn't the first time I've made love,' she told him stingingly.

His calm, 'I know,' silenced her; and as she bent her head over her cup of tea she knew that her face was burning.

'Your daughter rang. I told her you were still asleep. She sounds very mature for her age.'

Her heart almost stopped. She had picked up her cup, but now she returned it to its saucer with a betraying clatter.

'She is.' Her voice shook and so did her body.

'She sounds very like you,' Silas added softly.

He couldn't begin to describe to her what he had felt like hearing that childish voice and recognising in it the more mature tones of the woman he loved. He ached to be able to tell her how much he wished he had been the one to give her her child, but he hadn't been and he never would be. And he hadn't sunk quite so low yet, thank God, that he was prepared to use the sexual chemistry between them to force her into a relationship which would mean that she would never be able to have the family she had always wanted.

He remembered them talking about it . . .

'Oh, I'd want at least four children,' she had told him confidently, and he had smiled at her, already picturing her swollen with his child, already anticipating how he would feel when he held their first-born.

She would give him sons, she had told him proudly, and he had told her he would prefer girls.

Now there would be neither.

A contagious infection . . . poor medical attention . . . a diagnosis made far too late, and the result was that for him there would never be any children.

If he told her . . . But he knew how much having a family meant to her, and he couldn't bear to see her shrink from him in horror and pity.

A man who couldn't father a child. He felt the sweat break out on his skin, and cursed. He had thought himself over that particular mental hurdle long ago; all it had taken to show him that he wasn't was having the warmth of the woman he loved in his arms; of filling her flesh with his own in that most intimate of physical unions; of hearing her cries of pleasure as he took her to the highest peaks of delight.

Had she cried out with joy the night she had conceived her lover's child?

Her lover . . . Who had he been, the man who had fathered that bright-voiced little girl who had spoken to him so confidently and gravely? Where was he now? He didn't want to think about it, and so he turned abruptly on his heel and walked back to the door.

Kate let him go. Even now she couldn't regret last night; her body still pulsed slightly in the aftermath of their pleasure. If he had chosen to stay, to touch her . . . The tiny quivers of sensation within her became fierce darts that made her catch her breath.

She must forget about last night, she told herself sternly. She must get up and ring Cherry. She must keep herself busy, so that her enforced stay here would soon pass and she would be free to return to reality and forget this brief span of time here with Silas.

She had intended to go over to the main building to see if she could help out immediately after she had had her breakfast, but when she rang the farm she discovered that Cherry was out with her father and so she decided to stay in the house until she returned, even though her mother assured her that she was feeling more cheerful.

'Your father's taking her up to Sam Benson's this afternoon,' she told her.

Sam Benson was a neighbouring farmer who was her father's keenest rival at the sheep-dog trials. Her father didn't approve of the methods Sam used to train his dogs, considering that the other man verged on being too harsh.

'He's teaching her to play chess as well,' her mother told her with a chuckle.

Chess was her father's favourite game, although he didn't get much opportunity to play. He had taught both her and David when they were younger. David hadn't liked the game, being too impatient, but she had quite enjoyed it. She had played it with Silas, although she was by no means as skilled at it as he was.

'She already knows the rudiments,' she told her mother.

Kate had discerned quite early in her daughter's life that she had an aptitude for both maths and music—gifts she had acquired through her father, Kate suspected.

It was late morning before Kate could speak to Cherry herself. As her mother had said, Cherry sounded far happier than she had done the previous evening. She was full of excited chatter about her morning, but broke off to ask Kate, 'Who was that man I spoke to before? He was nice.'

'Oh, that's the man who runs the centre,' Kate told her huskily, praying that her daughter would never have cause to know how much she was lying to her, if only by default.

'Cherry seems mightily taken with whoever it was who answered the telephone this morning,' her mother confirmed, when Cherry handed over the telephone to her grandmother.

'It's the man who runs the centre. Silas Edwards,' Kate told her in a strained voice.

'Edwards, you say?' her mother queried, repeating Silas's surname, and then Kate heard her saying to her father, 'Isn't that the man who's bought Jessop's farm, John?'

Kate heard her father's reply quite clearly, and her stomach was still churning when she replaced the receiver. She remembered someone saying Silas had bought a farm locally. There must be a hundred reasons why Silas had bought the farmland that ran adjacent to their own, but she couldn't think of a single one. Why, when he had told her himself that he was dedicated to his career and the worldwide travelling it involved, had he bought himself a remote hill farm?

She was still trying to puzzle out the answer when the phone rang again.

She picked it up automatically, giving the number. There was silence from the other end, and then a woman's voice, crisp and light, enquiring coolly, 'I'm sorry, I'm not sure whom I'm speaking to.'

'Kate Seton,' Kate told her, trying to sound equally calm, while her heart thumped madly as her senses picked up on the undercurrent of surprised hostility in the other woman's voice. Who was she? A friend? A lover? A woman who had far more right to be here in Silas's home than she did herself? That thought hurt.

'Seton?' The voice sharpened again. There was a pause, and then she said briskly, 'I wonder if you'd give Silas a message for me. Could you tell him that Susie rang? Oh, and that we'll be coming up with the boys as planned, but that I'll get in touch with him before then.'

Susie . . . the boys . . . Kate's heartbeat started to ease a little.

She had jumped to erroneous conclusions once before in the past with disastrous consequences; this time she would be wise to be more cautious.

Could this Susie be Silas's sister? What had he said she was called?

Since it was almost time for lunch, there seemed little point in going to the centre. Instead, she opened the fridge and made herself a light snack from the food her mother had sent.

After that she collected her own washing, and, after a moment's hesitation, Silas's as well. It seemed churlish not to when all she had to do was to put it in the machine.

Odd how, even in these progressive days, to do a man's laundry was a sign of intimacy.

Half-way through the afternoon exhaustion overwhelmed her, and when Silas came back at five o'clock he found her fast asleep in an armchair.

She looked young and vulnerable, and he ached to touch her. By rights, he ought still to be working, but he hadn't been able to concentrate. All he had been able to think about was Kate. Kate now . . . Kate then. Kate who had followed him all through the years, haunting him, and who haunted him now.

Unable to stop himself, he reached out and touched her hair, letting a soft curl slide through his fingers.

As he bent over her, Kate woke up. For a moment she was confused and disorientated and she reached up to him, her face radiant with joy, only to remember abruptly that this was now, and the days when she had had the right to reach out towards him were long gone.

To Silas, her abrupt withdrawal was another

sign that, although physically she desired him, he was not the man she loved, and so he stepped back from her himself, his face closed and shadowed.

'Don't get up,' he told her curtly as she started to move. 'I only came back to get some papers.'

It was a lie, but it would be easier to go back and attempt to do some of the work he should have already done than to stay here with her.

He was half-way out of the door before Kate remembered to give him his message.

'Yes, my sister and her family. They're planning to spend a few days with me en route for their annual holiday in Scotland.'

'I'm surprised you want to be bothered with them,' Kate challenged him, 'in view of the way you feel about family life.'

The look he gave her was bleak. If that was what she wanted to think, why should he disillusion her? For the sake of his pride, it was better that she should believe he didn't want to be a father rather than know the truth. Had she been a different sort of woman, a woman to whom children weren't important, he could perhaps . . .

Perhaps what? Beg her to love him as he had once believed she did? As he closed the front door behind him, his face contorted in harsh lines of pain.

CHAPTER EIGHT

A WEEK. One week . . . Over now, and yet it had seemed more like a lifetime. Or at least parts of it had, Kate acknowledged, trying not to remember those hours in Silas's arms that had passed like as many seconds.

And now, this afternoon, she would be free to leave. She was probably already free to leave. So why was she hesitating before ringing her father to tell him that she was ready? Why was she standing here in Silas's kitchen, staring down the drive, almost as though she was willing him to appear?

Why should he? Common sense told her that he must be eager for her to go. What had happened between them—well, that was something it seemed they both wanted to forget. And yet he had wanted her so much. Surely she hadn't been wrong about that?

She reminded herself how small her experience really was, and how easily she could have read more into Silas's response to her than there actually had been, simply out of her own mind.

Cherry would be waiting for her at the farm. Cherry. A frown touched her forehead. For the last two days her daughter had seemed very subdued. Her parents had noticed it as well, but neither of them had been able to give Kate any explanation for it, other than to say that she was probably missing her.

But Kate, with a mother's instinct, knew it was something more. Cherry hadn't guessed the truth, surely? Her heart missed a beat and then steadied. Of course not. How could she? No, it would be some small, childish problem that was darkening her daughter's life and displacing the joy from her voice.

She glanced at her watch. It was five o'clock. Silas wouldn't come now. She reached out to pick up the telephone and call her father.

'Kate . . .'

She spun round in shock. Silas must have walked back to the house along the path that curled through the park, and that was why she hadn't seen him.

'I'm just ringing my father to ask him to come and pick me up,' she told him formally, avoiding looking directly at him. If she did, he would have to see in her eyes how she felt about him, and that was the last thing she wanted.

'I'll drive you home,' he told her roughly. 'Just give me half an hour to shower and change.'

'There's no need——' she began.

But he overruled her, saying savagely, 'There's every need,' and her heart jerked at the raw sound of the words as though he had actually pulled its strings, as though the need he spoke of was that elemental fierce pulse that kept her awake at night.

When he came downstairs his hair was still damp, and where his shirt touched his skin the fabric had darkened slightly, as though beneath its covering his skin was still moist.

The thought made her body go weak, and she turned away from him hastily.

'I'll just go up and get my things . . .'

'I'll bring them down for you.'

Sighing faintly, Kate walked into the kitchen. Her cases weren't heavy and she could quite easily have carried them herself, but she admitted that there was something rather pleasant about being female and cosseted on occasions.

Even so, she insisted on carrying one of them out to the Range Rover and helping Silas to load them. His movements were deft and assured. He was the sort of man a woman would always feel comfortable with: protected by his masculinity but never threatened by it. He was male, without being macho.

'All set.'

He wasn't looking at her, she saw, checking out of the corner of her eye, and so she hesitated for a fraction of a minute, looking at the house, wanting to imprint it on her memory. It wasn't a particularly attractive building, but it was here that she and Silas had come together, and she would always remember it with an ache of sadness.

'Kate . . .'

She hadn't heard him move, and when she felt his hand cupping her elbow she jumped. His grip tightened, his breath warm against her skin as he asked curtly, 'Is something wrong?'

She was a woman, not a girl, Kate reminded herself, pinning a bright smile to her face as she turned to meet the look in his eyes.

'No. Nothing.'

And then, turning, she pulled away from him and walked firmly towards the waiting Range Rover.

Neither of them spoke again until they were through the gates. The sight of the small flock of sheep grazing freely in the parkland made Kate say, 'You must be pleased that the new breed is turning out so well. Graham was telling me that it was your idea originally to try a new high-yield, low-disease-prone strain.'

'It's too early to congratulate ourselves yet,' was Silas's curt response. 'And certainly far too early to expect the Ministry to give full approval. But so far . . . yes, I am pleased.'

'So how long will it be before they can actually breed them in places like Ethiopia?' Kate asked him.

'Three years, maybe two if we're lucky,' he told her shortly.

'So how long will it be before you go back there?' Kate asked him miserably. All at once it was too much of an effort to pretend any longer. In many ways it would have been less cruel of fate to have ensured that they had never met again, rather than for her to have to suffer the anguish of knowing exactly what she had really lost all those years ago.

At eighteen she had loved Silas as a girl of that age does: hedonistically, sensuously, selfishly in many ways. Now she realised that she loved him with a mature woman's love, recognising his integrity and compassion, his strength and his vulnerability.

Wrapped in her own thoughts, she didn't see the expression that crossed his face. Go back . . . In many ways he wished he could, but the illness he had suffered had left him with a physical vulnerability that meant that he could not be pronounced medically fit for such gruelling work. Field work in places such as Ethiopia was barred to him, which was why . . .

He looked at Kate and saw that she was waiting for his response.

Her eyes looked anxious and strained. No doubt she was regretting their lovemaking, perhaps even fearing that he might be contemplating continuing their relationship. For her sake if nothing else, he ought to reassure her, and so he lied and told her, 'Not long.'

They were almost at the farm. Kate could see the familiar outline of it and then they were driving into the yard, scattering the hens and geese, and Cherry was opening the back door and running toward them.

Surely Cherry had grown? Her jeans seemed too short for her long legs, and her skin was tanned a healthy country brown from the long hours she had spent outside with her grandfather. She greeted Kate rapturously, and then turned from her mother to study Silas.

Kate felt her heart pound with dread as they looked at one another. Would Silas see himself in their child, as she so often did?

Apparently not. Gravely, formally, he extended his hand and shook Cherry's small, grubby paw.

'Gran says you're to hurry up and come inside because she's just brewed some tea,' Cherry announced forthrightly, and somehow or other Kate found that, instead of politely thanking Silas and watching him drive out of her life, the three of them were walking into her mother's cosy kitchen.

She saw Silas looking round appreciatively, and tried to see the room through his eyes. It was so familiar to her that she tended to overlook its appeal.

It was a large, rectangular room, which would have been dark if it hadn't been for the benefit of electric light. The walls were old and almost two feet deep, the stone mullioned windows small, and during the summer her mother normally kept the back door open to allow in more light.

The floor still had its ancient flags, and the rag rugs that Kate remembered from her own childhood and which she remembered her mother telling her had been made by her grandmother.

The oak units, the kitchen's only relatively modern touch, had been made by her father one bad winter from wood he had seasoned himself, and he was justifiably proud of them. The scrubbed table was several hundred years old, but her mother swore that it was impossible for her to make pastry on anything else.

The Aga was a new one, replacing the ancient model Kate remembered; it was also fire-engine red, a colour her mother had confessed she had fallen in love with in the shop.

The old-fashioned wing-chairs either side of it were slightly shabby. Kate remembered that her mother had been threatening to re-cover them for years. She herself was a clever needlewoman, and she made a mental note to find out what kind of fabric her mother had in mind and to take over the task for her as a small thank-you for all that she was doing for Cherry and herself. She could also make her some new curtains while she was here, Kate mused, and the walls could do with a fresh coat of paint.

Living on her own on a teacher's salary, she had quickly learned how to make the most of her small home, and, although she didn't consider herself to be artistic in the strict sense of the word, she enjoyed being creative with her home—a gift that Cherry had inherited from her.

Here, though, there were differences. Her mother's kitchen bore very evident signs of male occupation of the house; small things that were missing from her own home. It bothered her at times that Cherry was growing up without any male influence on her life, and she was pleased that her daughter had struck up such a bond with her father.

As she was thinking about him, the latter came in. Since it was extremely rare for him to be off the fells at this time of the day during the summer, Kate suspected that he had come deliberately to inspect Silas. She was touched and amused, and then wryly surprised at her reaction, remembering the many, many rows that had taken place in this very kitchen when she was in her early teens because of her parents' insistence on vetting the young men she went out with.

Now she found it touching that her father should take such a protective interest in her.

'It is good of you to bring Kate back, Mr Edwards,' her mother began, smiling warmly when Silas offered,

'Please call me Silas, Mrs Seton. And as for being good . . .' He gave a wry grimace. 'I felt I could hardly do less in view of the fact that it was our work at the institute which was responsible for your daughter's incarceration.'

'Well, not entirely,' her mother chuckled. 'There was, after all, Annabel's part in it.'

'Annabel? Oh yes, of course, the goat,' Silas agreed.

'I see you've got some sheep grazing in the paddocks. Are they Merinos . . .' her father asked Silas sharply.

Kate held her breath, wondering how he would answer her father's question. Her father knew all there was to know about sheep and their breeding, and Kate suspected that he was quite well aware that those grazing on the paddocks were different from his own prize flock.

'Not exactly,' Silas answered him easily. 'They're a new breed we're hoping to introduce, but as yet their development is only in the very early stages.' As he went on to explain the technical details to her father, adding that it was the tests they were carrying out on the flock that had been responsible for the quarantine problems,

Kate was torn between pleasure at seeing the man she loved getting on so well with her parents, and pain because no one other than herself would ever know of the very special relationship he had with them, especially with Cherry.

She looked at her daughter, and saw that she was sitting staring at Silas, totally enraptured, her small face propped up in her hands as she leaned on the table and watched him.

'Do you have any dogs to look after your sheep?' she asked him seriously at length.

Kate felt her heart leap into her throat, and her eyes burn with emotional tears as she looked at them. Father and daughter, and to her, if no one else, so very alike. More, perhaps, in small ways than obvious ones, and her throat locked tight with love and pain as Silas replied equally gravely, 'No, we don't, I'm afraid . . .'

'I could lend you Blackie,' Cherry offered. 'He's my dog, and I'm training him, but he's only a pup yet. But he's got the makings . . .'

To his credit, Silas didn't smile.

'I could show him to you if you like,' Cherry offered.

The kitchen had become oddly silent, and Kate was so totally engrossed in watching Silas and Cherry that it was several seconds before she realised her parents were watching her. Once she did realise, a vivid flush stained her face. What had she given away in those few unguarded seconds to bring that look to both their faces?

'I'd like that very much,' she heard Silas saying, and Cherry got up, offering him information about

her pup and its training in the slightly old-
fashioned way she had picked up from Kate's
father.

'Are you coming with us, Mum?' Cherry
invited, but Kate shook her head. She didn't think
she was strong enough to withstand the emotional
impact of watching them together—father and
daughter, although neither of them knew it. And
Silas was so good with her, seeming to know by
instinct how to treat her. How not to talk down to
her, because Cherry was at that vulnerable age
when she was just beginning to be aware of adult
condescension and hurt by it. But then, of course,
he would have his experience with his sister's sons
to guide him.

She watched them walk across the yard
together, Cherry looking up at Silas as she chatted
energetically to him.

'Does he know . . . about Cherry?' her mother
asked quietly from behind her, making her stiffen
and turn to look at her in shock.

'How . . . how did you know?' she stammered,
looking from her mother's face to her father's and
seeing the truth on both of them.

'She's very like him,' her mother said quietly.
'And besides, we're your parents. He seems very
nice,' she added inconsequentially, and Kate's
heart ached, because in her mother's voice she
heard the concern of mothers the world over, for
their children and their happiness.

'He is,' she agreed softly. 'But no, he doesn't
know, and I can't tell him. For Cherry's sake.' She
had never really explained to her parents what had

happened, and she did so now, not sparing herself when describing how she had seen Silas with his sister and children and immediately leapt to the wrong conclusion.

'We've talked quite a lot this last week, and one thing I have learned is that Silas does not want the encumbrance of a wife and family. He told me so himself, and I can't take the risk of having Cherry hurt by discovering that he's her father, only to find out that he doesn't want her.

'Even though you still love him.'

'Even though I still love him,' Kate confirmed. 'Even though I love him far more than I ever did before.'

Silas didn't leave until well into the evening. He fitted well into her family, Kate recognised, listening to him discussing the various merits of selective breeding with her father.

'It's all very well in theory,' her father half scoffed, 'but wait until you have to put it into practice.'

'I quite agree,' Silas responded. 'And I'll soon have an opportunity to find out just how successful this new strain is. I've bought a farm not far from here. It's very neglected and run-down at present, and the land needs attention, but when I officially leave my present post at the end of the summer I hope to concentrate on seeing just how this new strain develops . . .'

Kate stared at him, her heart thudding uncomfortably, totally ignoring everyone else as she challenged huskily, 'How can you do that?

You said you were going back to Ethiopia.'

Silas looked at her, breaking off his conversation with her father. He had been so totally engrossed in what they were discussing and his own enthusiasm for the subject that he had allowed himself to be trapped in his own lies.

His throat went dry. He could see anger in Kate's eyes, and pain as well, and his pulses started to pound. Could it be possible that, despite everything, she still cared for him?

Of course she did. She must. She could never have made love with him the way she had the other night if she didn't.

But giving way to the overwhelming sentiment of the moment was one thing, making a lifelong commitment was another, and he knew he couldn't bear the thought of Kate turning away from him in pity when she learned the truth. His pride, and his fear that her compassion for him would lead her into sacrificing herself to a relationship which would be devoid of the family she had so often stated she wanted, would not allow him to tell her how much he loved and needed her.

He had quickly learned from Cherry's bright chatter when she showed him her pup that she had no knowledge or experience of her father, but that was not to say that at some stage he might not appear to share their lives. Kate still loved him. She had said so.

'Yes . . . Yes, I am,' he lied. 'I'll be getting a manager for the farm.'

By the time she discovered the truth, she would be back in London, and he would do all he could to ensure that on her future visits home he kept out of her way.

They all went out into the yard to see him off, Kate's father gruffly telling him that he was welcome to call whenever he chose.

He was just about to get into the Range Rover when, to everyone's surprise, Cherry rushed up to him and hugged him briefly.

He held on to her automatically, bending his head to ruffle her hair and return her embrace.

She was tall for an eight-year-old, he thought, her coltish body promising elegance in adulthood, but she was still young enough and obviously loved enough to be totally natural with everyone.

After he had gone and they went back in the kitchen, Cherry said wistfully, 'Silas is really nice. I wish . . .'

'What?' Kate demanded forcefully, staring at her, her whole body tense. Please God, don't let Cherry say she wished he was her father . . .

But she realised her imagination was working overtime when Cherry said simply, 'I wish we could stay here for ever, Mum, instead of going back to London. It's so much better up here.'

Kate didn't sleep well that night; the wind in the eaves disturbed her, and then later so did the silence. In fact, everything disturbed her, or was it just her own thoughts and memories that wouldn't allow her to sleep? Or perhaps the knowledge that Silas wasn't there?

In the morning she woke up with a headache that refused to go away.

After one look at her, her mother suggested that a morning spent weeding the vegetable garden might help.

'There's something very therapeutic about pulling out weeds, I always think. Perhaps it's the righteous vice of being destructive in a good cause. I always imagine I can hear the plants sighing in relief as I pull out the weeds.' She smiled whimsically at Kate, who tried to respond.

Her father was going to see Sam Benson and he was taking Cherry with him. As it wasn't far across the fields, they were going to walk.

They came back just before lunch. Kate, sitting back on her heels and surveying the neat pile of weeds she had extracted from the vegetable garden, watched them.

Cherry had her head down and her footsteps dragged. She was walking very stiffly several yards away from her grandfather's side, and it was plain to Kate that something was wrong.

She got up unsteadily. So far, her parents had not witnessed Cherry's very stubborn streak. Normally sunny-natured, her daughter could be astonishingly recalcitrant when she thought she had right on her side. Just like her father. And just like her grandfather, too, Kate reflected wryly, dusting down her jeans and going to meet them.

Cherry refused to meet her eyes, and so did

her father. Both of them looked mutinous. Both of them were glowering.

Kate waited until she and Cherry were safely upstairs before asking firmly, 'What's wrong?'

Cherry had her back to her as she washed her hands ready for lunch, and Kate took hold of her shoulders and firmly turned her round so that she could look at her. Ever since Cherry had been old enough to understand and reason for herself, Kate had accorded her daughter the same respect she would an adult, offering guidance and advice, but never imposing her own views on her.

Now she wondered if she had done the right thing, or if, perhaps, she had been too lax. Did Cherry trust her enough to tell her what was wrong, or would she believe that Kate must automatically side with her own father?

'I wanted Gramps to buy Meg—that's Mr Benson's dog—and bring her with us, but he wouldn't.'

Kate expelled a faint sigh of relief.

'Well, I expect he had a good reason for that, didn't he?'

'He said Meg belonged to Mr Benson and that we just couldn't take her.'

'Well, no,' Kate agreed, trying to feel her way through what she suspected was going to be a very dangerous minefield indeed.

'But poor Meg was tied up with no water and no food, and the chain had rubbed on her neck and . . .'

Cherry started to cry, and Kate bit her lip,

knowing how her daughter felt about the ill-treatment of animals, any animals . . .

'I wanted Gramps to bring Meg away. I would have paid Mr Benson for her, but Gramps said he couldn't interfere with the way a man treats his dog. And then he frowned at me, you know the way he does, and said we had to come home. And poor Meg cried, Mum. It was awful.'

Kate sighed again. She could see it all. Her father was a farmer, with a farmer's lack of sentiment about animals, but Cherry was still a child, with ideals and a very tender heart. In Cherry's eyes, her grandfather had failed her, and in her father's eyes, Cherry was probably making a fuss about nothing, Kate reflected, knowing how much her father detested what he called 'women's softness'.

It took her a while to persuade Cherry to go down for lunch, but when they got there she found that Kate's father had been in and gone out again.

Over Cherry's head, Kate and her mother exchanged understanding looks, both of them trying to distract the little girl as she toyed with food she obviously didn't want, her small face pale and strained.

Kate's headache, which had started to abate during the morning, had returned in a full-blown migraine, and when, after lunch, Cherry asked if she could go out and play, Kate agreed.

It was her mother's day for her local WI meeting, and with her head throbbing so painfully that she could hardly see, Kate went upstairs to lie down.

At some time or another she must have fallen asleep, because the next thing she knew was when her mother shook her gently awake and proffered a cup of tea.

'I can't have slept so long,' Kate groaned, sitting up. Her headache had gone, leaving her feeling weak and slightly lethargic as it always did. 'How's Cherry now?'

'I don't know. I haven't seen her,' her mother told her. She saw Kate's face and soothed, 'Now, don't start to panic. I've only just driven in, and I came straight inside. It's only half-past five, and I told her we wouldn't be eating until later today because I was going out. She's a sensible child, Kate, and unlikely to do anything foolish.'

'But she *is* a child,' Kate responded, 'and I'm her mother . . .' She pushed back the bedclothes. 'Where on earth can she be?'

'Look, before you start panicking, I'll go down and check the yard. She's probably out with Blackie. She normally takes him out around this time for his training.'

Conceding that her mother was right, Kate nevertheless dressed quickly and followed her downstairs.

As her mother had predicted, Cherry's pup was missing. 'Why don't you go to the end of the lane and give her a shout? She never takes him very far,' she suggested.

Kate followed her advice, terrified of admitting the fear growing inside her. One read such

dreadful news items about missing children.
Cherry might be sensible, but she was only ten
years old . . .

She called her name until her throat was sore,
and then, just when she was beginning to panic
in earnest, she saw Cherry running towards her,
over the crest of the hill, Blackie at her heels.

She was breathless by the time she reached
Kate, her face flushed, and an oddly guilty look
in her eyes, but Kate was too relieved to see her
to do anything more than say chidingly, 'Where
on earth have you been? I've been calling you for
ages.'

'I was walking Blackie.'

An averted profile muffled the explanation
slightly, and, taking a firm grip of her arm, Kate
led her back towards the farmhouse.

Over tea, Cherry was subdued, but Kate put it
down to the fact that she was still hurt by her
grandfather's refusal to rescue the dog.

Even so, she was surprised to hear Cherry
saying at seven o'clock that she was tired, and
went upstairs with her while she got ready for
bed, anxious to make sure there was nothing
really wrong.

'Gramps would have helped if he could, I'm
sure,' she told Cherry as she tucked her up. 'But
he could hardly just take Mr Benson's dog, could
he?'

Cherry went white and averted her face, her
mouth trembling, and Kate sighed. There were
times when her daughter could be so sensitive.
As she smoothed back her hair from her fore-

head, she told herself that she had been wise not to say anything about Cherry to Silas. It was better surely that Cherry shouldn't know her father, rather than that she should know him and be hurt by him.

'Is she all right?' Kate's mother asked when Kate went back downstairs.

'Not really. She's very upset about the dog.' Kate looked at her father and saw that he was scowling, a sure sign that he was embarrassed and uncomfortable. 'Is there really nothing we can do, Dad? She says the animal is being badly treated.'

'I offered to buy it off him, but he wouldn't sell.'

'But if it's being badly treated, surely the RSPCA . . .'

'This isn't the city,' her father interrupted harshly. 'Up here, it's still a man's own business how he treats his beasts.'

Kate sighed, knowing there was nothing more she could say or do, other than perhaps to try to have a word with the vet to see if there was anything *he* could do.

None of them heard or saw the small, slim figure creeping stealthily down the rear staircase and out into the yard. Blackie started to yelp as he recognised his young mistress, but Cherry silenced him quickly.

It was a long way to the disused farm where she had hidden the dog. It greeted her with yelps similar to Blackie, jumping up to lick her face, as she kneeled down to give it the food she had brought for it.

She dared not stay long, and she hated the mournful way the dog howled as she left.

'Gone, they are, and I can't find them anywhere,' Kate heard her father grumble.

'What's gone?' she asked him as she walked across the yard. There was still a certain coolness between Cherry and her grandfather; the former having gone off by herself this morning for a walk.

'A brand new pair of wire-cutters.'

'Oh, well, I expect they'll turn up,' Kate comforted him, her mind more on Cherry than on her father's missing wire-cutters.

Over lunch, Cherry was still very subdued. She looked pale, there were shadows under her eyes and her normal bright smile was dimmed, and when Kate's father asked her if she wanted to go down to the village with him she shook her head.

It was the postman the following morning who brought them the news.

'Have you heard about Sam Benson's missing dog?' he asked chattily, as he handed over the letters to Kate.

She shook her head, her body suddenly chilling.

'Seems someone's gone and stolen it. Mad as fire he is.' He looked speculatively around the yard. 'Seems to think your father might have had something to do with it . . . Claims he wanted to buy the dog.'

Kate tried to look surprised, knowing that whatever she said was all too likely to be passed on to the next farm he delivered to, and then went inside, handing over the mail to her mother. Cherry was sitting huddled over her breakfast, and it was barely touched.

Kate looked at her daughter. Surely it was stretching her imagination too far to think that Cherry was responsible for the dog going missing?

Even so, as soon as she could, she got Cherry on her own and sat her down on the windowseat of the bedroom that had been Kate's own when she was a girl.

'Mr Benson's dog is missing,' she told Cherry, without preamble, 'and he's virtually accusing your grandfather of being responsible.'

She had her hands on Cherry's shoulders, and she felt her flinch and her own heart dropped.

'Cherry, you must tell me. Did you take the dog?'

Cherry hung her head, her voice muffled by tears as she said huskily, 'Yes. I had to, Mum,' she added defiantly, her eyes flashing as her head came up. 'She's frightened of him and so thin . . .'

'But, Cherry, that's stealing.'

Kate cursed herself for her unthinking words as she saw Cherry go white.

'I thought she was chained up,' she said in a softer tone. 'How did you set her free?'

'I took the wire-cutters. I worked it all out . . .'

'And where is she now?' Kate asked her, hardly able to believe what she was hearing.

'The old Jessop farm. The one that Mr Edwards has bought. I've shut her in one of the barns there. Mum, will I go to prison?'

Tears filled her eyes and ran down her cheeks, and for all her fear and anger Kate couldn't stop herself from taking her in her arms and hugging her reassuringly.

'Of course not. But what you did was wrong, Cherry. Yes, I know you felt you were right. I understand why you did it, but if you'd just waited a little while I was going to ask the vet if there was anything he could do. The dog will have to be returned to Mr Benson, you must see that . . .'

And, knowing of the local rivalry between her father and Mr Benson, who was going to believe that a ten-year-old had been responsible for the dog's theft, especially in the tough farming community of the Dales?

If the truth came out, it would damage the reputation for straight dealing of which her father was so proud, but they couldn't keep the dog hidden away for ever . . .

'What are you going to do?' Cherry asked her mother tearfully.

In all honesty, it was a relief to tell her what she had done. The strain of the long walk to and from the uninhabited farm twice a day, the food she had to carry, the fear that something would happen to Meg when she wasn't there had all weighed heavily on her, and she looked trust-ingly at Kate, waiting for her response.

'Well, I think the first thing I have to do is to find some way of getting Meg back to Mr Benson without him knowing who took her. Then we'll try and find a way to make sure that he takes proper care of her in future!'

She dared not promise any more, not even sure if she could accomplish even that much.

And as for returning the dog . . . How on earth was that to be achieved? The same way in which she had been removed in the first place, Kate suspected. And surely if a ten-year-old child could do it, then so could a twenty-nine-year-old woman.

'Dry your eyes,' she told Cherry. 'And then I think you and I had better go for a walk. I think it might be as well if you introduced me to Meg before I try smuggling her back into Mr Benson's yard.'

CHAPTER NINE

'A WALK, at this time of night?' Kate's father scowled at her. He had been in an irritable mood all evening, and for one dreadful moment Kate felt as though she were seventeen again, with her father having the power to veto her movements.

'It's going to rain,' he added growlingly. 'A walk!'

'It helps me to sleep,' Kate told him calmly, refusing to allow her inner agitation to show.

Somehow or other she had to get that dog back to its rightful home without anyone knowing what had happened. Guiltily, she tried not to remember the forlorn look in Cherry's eyes when she had told her what she intended to do.

The sun which had warmed the Dales ever since their arrival had deserted them during the afternoon, and as she went outside Kate shivered in the cold wind that rushed across the yard.

Her London coat was no protection against its icy chill, and for a second she hesitated, debating whether or not to go back and get something warmer. She had a thick sweater upstairs. But if she went back, her father would probably delay her, and it was already late enough.

Hunching her shoulders against the wind, she set off along the track which cut across the fields in the direction of Jessop's farm.

The clouds made the landscape cold and dark, and she wished she had had the foresight to bring a torch with her. As she neared the farm, the dog started to bark—a shrill, demanding noise that tensed her nerve-endings. She prayed that her father wasn't outside to hear it. She knew quite well how sound carried around the Dales, and how one dog could pick up the bark of another miles away and repeat it.

Her father, with his Dalesman's ear, would soon realise where the sound was coming from, and knowing that Jessop's farm was empty might be tempted to come and investigate, and that was the last thing she wanted.

She crossed the empty yard quickly, cursing mildly as her foot caught against an ancient piece of machinery. Farmers were notorious for refusing to dispose of antiquated equipment.

Cherry had told her that she had shut the dog in the barn, and as she drew nearer to it the animal's barking increased.

It took Kate several minutes to open the heavy, rain-warped door, but at least it yielded, swinging heavily against her body and bumping her hip-bone. She yelped in pain and then dashed inside as the first heavy drops of rain began to fall.

Cherry, far better organised that she was herself, had left a torch on the bench just inside the door, and Kate switched it on in relief.

It was almost dark now, and the barn was dim. It smelled of musty hay—a familiar scent from her childhood.

As she switched on the light, the dog cowered

nervously. It was a pretty-looking animal with what promised in adulthood to be a long coat. She had the dainty feet of her breed and a small, quivering, pointed nose.

She and Kate eyed one another for a few seconds. Cherry had been thoughtful in her care of her, Kate recognised: there were two large bowls of fresh-looking water, and another of biscuits. The chain which tethered the dog was attached to one of the special soft collars that her father always used.

As Kate approached, the dog crouched down, beating her tail grovellingly on the dusty floor.

She was timid, Kate recognised as she cringed back from her; she was thin as well, and as Kate reached out to let her sniff her hand and then to stroke her, she found the ridges of old scars beneath her coat.

At heart she was as vulnerable as her daughter, and she ached to be able to do something for the dog, but she knew the Dales and its inhabitants far better than Cherry. It was an unwritten rule that no one interfered between a man and his dog, or a man and his wife, for that matter.

Once she realised that Kate wasn't going to hurt her, the dog stopped cringing and even tentatively licked her hand.

What on earth was she going to do? She had to take her back, Kate knew, and yet she hated the thought of returning the timid creature to her owner.

But if she didn't . . . This was a country dog, used to space and freedom, who would never adapt to city life. She and Cherry couldn't take her back to London with them.

Unhappily, she unfastened the chain and slipped on the lead that Cherry had left on the bench with the torch.

'I'm sorry about this, Meg, but I've got to do it,' she whispered sadly against the smooth head as the dog tried to snuggle up against her.

She was little more than half-grown, and her eyes beseeched Kate not to desert her.

She could feel her determination wavering, and then to her horror she heard a car coming up the road towards the farm. Quickly she doused the torch, hugging Meg to her. With a bit of luck it would just be someone going past, but it wasn't. She heard the engine note change and then slow down, and she knew that the driver had turned off to come to the farm.

The thought struck her that the driver might actually be her father, alerted by his own dogs to the fact that there was someone here.

If it was, she was going to have a very difficult interview in front of her.

The car stopped. She heard a door open and then slam. Meg whined, but Kate had her hand over her muzzle and she bent her head to whisper. 'Shush . . .'

As she did so, the barn door opened and someone shone a flashlight right into her eyes.

She gasped and lifted her hand instinctively to shield herself from the bright light.

'Kate, what the hell are you doing here?'

Silas! Kate went weak with relief.

Probably as much to his astonishment as to her own, as he let the barn door close against the rain she dropped the dog's lead and ran towards him, saying shakily, 'Thank God it's only you . . .'

'Who did you think it was?'

His arms had opened automatically to catch hold of her, and now they had closed around her, holding her against the comforting, solid weight of his body. Her head seemed to incline naturally against his shoulder. It was odd how at home she felt here in Silas's arms, Kate reflected dreamily.

'Kate, what are you doing here?' Silas persisted when he got no response.

It had been a shock to find her in his barn. Since he had bought the farm, he had had scant opportunity to spend much time on it. It was thoroughly run-down and needed a good deal of time and money investing in it. In three months' time, when his existing contract ran out, he planned to come and live here, putting into practice his research work.

Now that their quarantine was over, most of the staff were taking the opportunity to have some leave; the house without Kate in it, but somehow haunted by her, had not been somewhere he wanted to stay, so on impulse he had decided to drive up to the farm. His sister and her family would want to have a look at it when they arrived, and he had suspected from his memories of it at the time of the auction that it was in no fit state to show anyone.

To see the faint light glimmering in the barn

had come as a shock, and at first he had thought perhaps some squatters had taken up residence. The last person he had expected to find had been Kate.

And now here she was in his arms, her face turned into his shoulder so that he was tormented by the feminine perfume of her.

'Kate,' he repeated roughly, dragging himself back to reality. 'What's going on?'

Hearing the sharpness in his voice, Meg barked shrilly, and before Kate could stop her she launched herself at Silas, worrying at his ankles.

'What the . . .'

Astonished, he looked down at the dog.

'She thinks you're attacking me,' Kate told him gravely.

'She's yours?'

He released Kate and bent down to reassure the dog, talking softly to her, and coaxing her gently to allow him to stroke her. 'Nice animal, but she's too thin.' He started to frown as he found the old scar tissue, and looked at Kate grimly.

'I wish she was ours,' Kate sighed. 'Unfortunately, she belongs to Sam Benson.'

'Sam Benson! So she's the dog that's gone missing from Holme Farm. I heard all about it in the village when I stopped to buy some milk. What the devil are you doing with her?'

'Cherry stole her,' Kate told him baldly. 'She went up there with Dad the other day and saw Meg being ill-treated. I knew the moment they came back that something was wrong. Cherry hasn't been brought up here, she doesn't understand that there's a very strict code about what is and isn't permissible. I'm afraid my father has rather fallen from his pedestal. When he refused to do anything about Meg, Cherry decided to take matters into her own hands. She stole out one night with a pair of Dad's wire-cutters, if you please, and then brought Meg up here. That was a couple of days ago, and she's been keeping her here ever since.'

'And now?' Silas asked her quietly. Watching her, he had seen the shadows of emotion play across her face: so sensitive and tender-hearted, so much the protective mother, and yet vulnerable herself at the same time. He felt a rush of anger against the man who should have been with her to help her carry the responsibility of their child.

'I've explained to Cherry that Meg must go back.' Betrayingly, her fingers tightened in the dog's ruff as it went and sat beside her. 'According to Sam Benson, she's a very valuable animal. Dad did try to buy her, but of course he wouldn't sell.'

'Well, she's certainly well-bred enough, but I shouldn't think she'd be much good with sheep. She's too timid. She'd make a good house dog, though.'

'Even if I let Cherry keep her, which I can't, we can't take her back to London with us, she'd hate it. Cherry wanted Dad to report Sam to the RSPCA, but of course that isn't the way things are done up here. I did wonder if I could have a word with the vet and get him to try and do something.'

Meg whined and put up a paw to get her attention, and Kate stroked her gently. Poor little thing! Already she felt like the very worst kind of traitor, taking her back.

'Come on,' Silas said abruptly. 'Let's get her in the Range Rover.'

Before Kate could say a word he scooped up Meg, lead and all, and shouldered open the barn door, leaving Kate with no alternative but to follow him.

'There's no need for you to get involved in this, Silas,' she protested breathlessly as she caught up with him.

It was raining hard now, lashing needles of rain that stung her skin and soaked her hair and jacket.

'Get in the car and stop arguing,' Silas told her as he opened his own door and deposited Meg inside. 'It's too wet to stand outside.'

It was, and reluctantly Kate climbed in beside him.

The Range Rover felt warm after the musty coldness of the barn, and already their breath was misting up the windows.

Silas switched on the engine, the windscreen wipers having to work at double speed to clear the rain.

'How exactly were you planning to return her?' Silas asked Kate, turning to look at her. The engine was running, but he made no move to put the vehicle in motion.

'The same way Cherry got her out,' she told

him ruefully. 'I'm told it isn't too difficult a task to unfasten one of the links on the chain Sam uses. I was hoping that when he discovered she'd been returned, he'd be too surprised to make further enquiries . . .'

She flushed under the glance Silas shot her. Twenty-nine years old, and in many ways as innocent of reality as her daughter, he mused.

'But surely the moment you tried to get into the yard his other dogs would have started barking. He does have other dogs, doesn't he?'

'Yes,' Kate agreed helplessly.

'So how did Cherry manage to get this one without alerting them?' he persisted.

Kate stared at him.

'I don't know,' she admitted.

It might be as well if he were to have a word with Cherry, Silas reflected grimly, and then caught himself up, reminding himself that he had no right to interfere. Cherry was not his child, and Kate had told him herself that she was still in love with the man who was her father.

'I've got a better idea,' he told her quietly, at last putting the Range Rover into gear and releasing the brake. Although Kate protested, he refused to tell her exactly what it was, and to her trepidation he headed instead for Holme Farm.

Just before they got there, he stopped and turned his head to look frowningly at Meg, and then, before Kate could stop him, he removed her collar and lead and, opening the door of the Range Rover, dragged her out into the pouring rain, despite Kate's furious protests.

'If this is your idea of solving the problem, then don't bother,' she told him hotly, following him out into the wet night, heedless of the fact that torrential rain was now soaking her hair and clothes.

Silas was still gripping Meg by her ruff. Dog and man were both as wet as she was herself, Kate realised, but she was too angry to care. If Silas thought by abandoning Meg that he was helping her, then he was way off course. She'd rather risk the wrath of a hundred Sam Bensons than turn the shivering little animal out into the night.

Mingling with her anger was a heavy sense of disillusionment; somehow she had expected better of Silas. She was not entirely unlike her daughter after all, she reflected wryly, although she was old enough to know the danger of putting fellow human beings up on pedestals.

'What do you think I'm going to do?' Silas asked her calmly, patently undisturbed by her flash of temper.

As he looked up at her from where he was scooping up mud and rubbing it into the wriggling dog's coat, rain splashed down on to his face, clinging to his eyelashes, making them damp and spiky.

Kate had an irresistible urge to reach down and run her fingertip along those lashes.

Heavens, what was the matter with her? she groaned inwardly. Here they were, standing in a rainstorm, and she in the middle of a row as well, and she was melting inside with wanting him.

'Abandon her,' she told him coldly.

'Wrong,' Silas responded with a small smile. 'Come on, you,' he said affectionately to Meg. 'I think that will do the trick, and don't you dare shake yourself all over me, either.'

'Now,' Silas said when they were all back in the Range Rover. 'You and I were on our way out for a drink together. This . . .' he turned to smile at Meg '. . . animal practically threw herself under our wheels. It's obvious to me that she's a stray. I think we should take her to the nearest RSPCA animal shelter, which I think is in Halston.'

'But that's nearly twenty miles away,' Kate breathed.

'So it is,' Silas agreed. 'I shall tell whoever's in charge that if the animal isn't claimed in the requisite time, I'm prepared to keep her myself.'

Kate stared at him.

'But where will you say we found her?'

'Oh, somewhere between here and Halston. Somehow, I doubt that Benson will even think of contacting the RSPCA to look for his lost dog, do you?'

Kate was overwhelmed, and her look told him so.

'But afterwards, when you bring her back . . . You *are* going to keep her, aren't you?' she demanded. 'You weren't just saying that . . .'

'Of course I'm going to keep her.' For the first time he sounded tense. 'And if Benson should try to claim her I shall simply tell him that I found her roaming and took her to the RSPCA . . . Which reminds me, after we've delivered her to her temporary home, I'd better get back to the barn and remove the evidence.'

'I'll come with you,' Kate told him, and then bit her lip. He had probably intended to drop her at home on his way to Halston, and now she had virtually invited herself to join him.

The smiling girl in charge of the shelter examined Meg carefully, and promised to get in touch with Silas if anyone came to claim her.

'She's a nice little thing, but so are they all. She looks like a farm dog. We don't get many of them in here, but I'll let you know if anyone claims her, and if they don't . . .'

'If they don't, I've got a home for her,' Silas told her firmly. 'Here's my card.'

Kate saw the girl's eyes widen as she looked at it. Looking at it herself, Kate saw why: there was an extremely impressive list of letters after Silas's name; confirmation that he had gone on to complete his PhD.

'Now for the barn.'

Despite the heat inside the Range Rover, Kate felt chilled to the bone when they eventually got back to the farm.

It was Silas who opened the barn door and carefully disposed of all evidence of the dog's occupation. She felt too drained to do anything more than stand helplessly and watch him.

As he finished, he looked up at her and said lightly, 'There's no need to look so worried. I don't believe they hang dog thieves any more.'

He had meant it as a joke, Kate knew that, but to her horror, instead of responding to him with an equally light-hearted comment, she burst into tears.

'Kate! Oh, God . . . Please don't . . . I'm sorry.'

The rough note of remorse in his voice did nothing to help her regain her self-control; instead it reminded her of those rare occasions in the past when she had wept and he had taken her in his arms to comfort her.

He did so now, cursing briefly, and then released her.

'We're both soaked. I've got some spare clothes in the farmhouse and the electricity's on. We can have a hot drink. Come on.'

She ought to protest that she could just as easily go home, but somehow or other she didn't.

The kitchen Silas ushered her into was more modern than her mother's, and she studied its gleaming units and expensive appliances in surprise.

'Not my idea,' Silas told her drily. 'This lot was installed by the previous owner. Personally, I prefer your mother's kitchen.'

'This would be all right if you changed these cupboard doors for something more in keeping. Oak . . . something like that,' Kate murmured, watching as he filled the kettle and switched it on.

'I've got some towels upstairs. I'll go and get them. No, you stay here,' he told her when she made to follow him. 'One thing the last owner did neglect to do was to repair the staircase, and it's very unsafe. I doubt if my spare jeans will fit you, but I've got a couple of shirts and sweaters up there which should at least prove drier than what you've got on.'

He wasn't gone long, barely long enough for Kate to look round the kitchen, and to mentally change the glossy melamine unit doors for the softer effect of wood, and equip the empty space in the middle of the room with a table similar to her mother's.

Where her mother had her Aga, this kitchen had a smaller wood-burning stove, and Kate was looking at it when Silas walked back in.

'Looks good, but doesn't work very well,' he commented wryly. 'This should help, though.'

He was carrying a portable fan heater, which he plugged into a socket, and within seconds Kate was enjoying its very welcome heat.

'Towel . . . shirt . . . sweater and socks,' Silas told her, passing her a bundle of clothes, and then, his back to her, he began to strip off his own wet things.

Kate couldn't move, transfixed by the rippling muscles of his back as he pulled off his sweater and removed his shirt. She heard him curse mildly as he struggled with the damp fabric of his jeans, and realised that she was staring at him.

Quickly she took off her jacket, hesitating as she started to unfasten her shirt.

Free of the encumbrance of his jeans, Silas turned round. His briefs were surely no more revealing than many a pair of swimming trunks, but her heart was suddenly thumping frantically, and the heat engulfing her body had nothing to do with that coming from the fan heater.

'Kate . . . Kate, are you all right?'

Her mouth had gone so dry, she couldn't even speak. She nodded and then shivered, caught in a tremor of awareness of how much she loved him.

Silas obviously mistook it for a shiver, and he caught hold of her, frowning chidingly as he touched her wet clothes.

'You're frozen,' he told her accusingly. 'Come on, let's get you into something dry and warm.'

And, as though she were Cherry's age, he flicked open the buttons of her blouse and tugged it off.

Where the rain had soaked through her shirt it had left damp patches on her skin. She wasn't wearing jeans, but a pleated skirt that was now soaking around the hem, and dutifully she stepped out of it as Silas unfastened the waistband.

It gave her an odd sense of *déjà vu* to look down at his dark head as he bent over the small task, and her stomach lurched protestingly as she remembered just when she had seen him like this before.

It had been late one evening. They had been out for a meal; she had been drinking rather more wine than usual and it had gone slightly to her head.

She had begged Silas to take her home with him, and once there she had begged him equally insistently to make love to her.

He had undressed her slowly, his hands trembling slightly, just as she was trembling now.

As he moved to stand up, he looked up at her, and saw the blind look of desire in her eyes.

The years rolled back; the way he said her name

was so familiar to her ears. She went eagerly into his arms, pressing her semi-naked body the length of his, feeling the muscles beneath his skin bunch as he gathered her to him, his hands in her hair as he held her still while he kissed her.

Her body melted against his with eager compliance, soft and yielding, and yet femininely demanding at the same time.

'Kate. . . Kate, we shouldn't be doing this,' Silas whispered against her mouth, but Kate didn't hear him and the sensation of her lips against his skin as she caressed him slowly, kissed her way down the arch of his throat, made him forget all the promises he made himself. She'd reached the curve of his shoulder now, and she was teasing him with little biting kisses—the kind he'd taught her when he showed what it was that gave pleasure to him. Although he tried to beat back the need rising within him, he couldn't resist lifting his hands to snap open her bra so that he could enjoy the rounded firmness of her breasts pressing against his chest.

Kate swayed dizzily as she felt him touch her, smooth the skin of her back, stroke her so that she arched up against him and then cried out beneath the deliberate friction of his body against hers, which was sensitising the already aroused hardness of her nipples.

She felt Silas move, lean back against the wall, taking her with him, gently easing her between his legs and then sliding his hands down over her back until he reached her hips.

There was very little she didn't know about his body, but the extent of his arousal startled her a little. In a teenager, eager for sexual experience and not totally at home with his body's reaction to desire, she could have understood it; but Silas was a man, well into his thirties, a man who, even when they had been lovers, had always appeared controlled.

Now, though . . . Now there was nothing controlled about him, she recognised, instinctively allowing her body to accommodate the arousal of his, as his hands gripped her hips and he moved roughly against her.

'Kate . . . Oh, God, what is it you do to me?'

He looked drawn and tired, like a man fighting with himself, Kate recognised.

'I want to make love to you. I *need* to make love to you, dammit,' he swore, but then, as she reached up to touch his face, he jerked away from her, the fierce thrust of his hips suddenly stilling, even though his body still pulsed hotly against her.

'Don't look at me like that. I don't want your pity.'

'You weren't being offered it,' Kate told him, stung by his abrupt change of mood. Her own body was aching tormentedly now, missing the enflaming movement of his, wanting more than the solid heat of him.

'No? What was I being offered, then?'

Kate stared at him, and then said shortly, 'Nothing.'

She tried to pull away from him, but he

wouldn't let her go.

'Kate . . . Kate, I'm sorry. That was an idiotic thing to say. Kiss and be friends?'

They were the same words he had said to her more than a lifetime ago, and, although she didn't want to hear them, she could feel her anger dissolving.

'All right,' she agreed weakly. 'Friends . . .'

'And the kiss?' Silas demanded huskily, and somehow or other his mouth was almost touching hers. *Was* touching hers, Kate realised in shock as the tender pressure of his lips suddenly became almost bruising, and he crushed her against him so that she could feel every tiny pulse thud of his blood, and almost felt she would drown beneath the flood of need that burst through her.

He kissed her mouth and her throat and her shoulder, and then with a groan picked her up and carried her over to the room's single chair, sitting down with her in his arms.

Kate wrapped herself around him, aching for his possession, hearing him groan, feeling the savage shudder that racked his body.

His mouth caressed her breasts. First one and then the other, opening over them and tugging on them, not gently as he had done before, but fiercely, so that she arched up helplessly against his mouth, lacing her fingers into his hair while she sobbed his name and felt the tiny pulsing points of pleasure buried deep inside her expand so quickly that she was caught off guard.

She opened her eyes and called out to him, her breath coming pantingly, and immediately his hand was on her body, easing, soothing, *satisfying* the fierce ache inside her long enough for him to remove the rest of their clothes and ease her down against him.

Her whole body vibrated with quivering anticipation as he entered her, easing himself into her slowly, as though he knew that to thrust too impatiently now would bring on the climax she was trying to hold at bay until she had tasted the pleasure of having him fully within her.

Kate closed her eyes and gave herself over to him, moving obediently to the stroke of his hands, arching her spine so that her nipples rubbed against his chest and she felt the betraying, quickened pulse of his flesh within her own. Already she was shivering with the knowledge of the pleasure to be, already her body was eagerly awaiting the sensations his flesh would unleash.

She felt him deep within her, filling her so completely that every sensitive nerve-ending was aware of him. With a soft groan she melted against him, closing her eyes, but Silas didn't move.

She waited tensely, and then opened her eyes to look at him.

'Silas.' She touched his mouth with her fingertips, her eyes enormous with arousal. 'I want you. I need you . . . now.'

'Show me.' His voice was rusty and thick, his eyes mirroring the glitter in her own. A tiny thrill shot through her, and wantonly she moved, rotating her hips, holding him, teasing him and then abruptly stopping, as she felt the powerful swell of her own need. Silas felt it too, and she cried out as he moved inside her.

They were lying on the floor, on Silas's damp clothes, and she felt one of the buttons on his shirt scrape her spine as Silas drove into her.

She cried out with pleasure at the sensation and gripped his sweat-slick back with her hands as her flesh dissolved in wave after wave of exquisite sensation.

When she opened her eyes, she discovered that she was lying several feet away on Silas's shirt. The rest of his clothes were some distance away and, as he followed the direction of her glance, she blushed furiously.

How had it happened? How had they come to make love so fiercely and passionately after everything she had told herself?

She already knew the answer. Or, at least, part of it. She loved him, and if it hadn't been for Cherry she would quite happily have abandoned everything else in her life to be with him, no matter how fleeting that time together might be.

But Cherry did exist, and Cherry's happiness was more important to her than her own. It had to be.

She started to wriggle away and Silas murmured softly, 'Stay with me . . .'

'I can't. My parents will be wondering where on earth I am.' She looked at her watch, dismayed to discover it was gone two in the morning. She hoped they'd gone to bed at their normally early time, and that they weren't worrying about her.

'Not just tonight . . .'

She looked at him, aching to reach out and touch him, but knowing that if she did she was lost.

'For how long, then? Until you go back to Ethiopia?' She forced herself to sound brisk. 'No, thanks, Silas.'

He drove her back to the farm in silence, and, although the dogs barked, no one stirred as she let herself in.

In the morning, her mother eyed her pale face and asked, 'What time did you get back last night? That must have been some walk . . .'

'I went up to Jessop's Farm. Silas was there and we got talking.'

Her head bent over her coffee-cup. She hoped her mother wouldn't see her burning face, but it seemed better to at least include some of the truth rather than lie completely.

CHAPTER TEN

ALMOST a week had gone by without a word from Silas. She *had* been expecting to hear from him, Kate acknowledged, if only to let her know about the dog.

Why *hadn't* he been in touch? Her mind produced all kinds of wild theories, including one that suggested that he might be lying ill at Jessop's farm, following a return of his fever, but before she could even think about going to check to see if she was right Cherry came looking for her to tell her that she had seen him in the village.

'He was with two other grown-ups and two boys,' she told Kate importantly, 'but he waved to me and said "hello".'

For someone she had virtually only met once, Cherry had formed a remarkable attachment to him, Kate reflected miserably.

Silas's companions must be his sister and her family, and Kate comforted herself with the thought that Silas was hardly likely to have time to get in touch with her if he had visitors.

She saw them all driving past the farm, when she went outside to help her mother pick the first of her early raspberries.

'Wasn't that Silas who just drove past?' her mother enquired, lifting her head just in time to see the disappearing Range Rover.

'Yes,' Kate told her repressively.

Taking the hint, her mother remained silent.

No doubt Silas was taking them to see the farm. She wondered idly who he had found to manage it while he was away, and from there it was only a short mental bridge to wondering how long it would be before he left. She shivered, her fingers stilling as she stared unseeingly into space.

'You know I won't be here this afternoon, don't you?' her mother asked, dragging her back to reality. It was her WI afternoon again.

'Yes, and Cherry's going off with Dad, so it looks like I'm going to be left on my own.'

'You could always come with me if you want to,' her mother told her briskly, but Kate shook her head.

'No, I won't, if you don't mind. I want to give Lydia a ring. I promised her I would before we left London, but somehow or other there just hasn't been the opportunity.'

'Oh, Kate.' Looking intensely guilty, her mother put her hand to her face in a gesture of dismay. 'How could I have forgotten? She rang while you were at the centre. You'll never guess what . . .'

'What?' Kate asked her curiously.

'She's thinking of getting married.'

'Lydia? But she's always said that a husband is the last thing she wants or needs.'

'Well she's obviously changed her mind. Nothing's settled yet apparently, but they're going on holiday together to the Seychelles, and they might even get married while they're out there. He's a widower, several years older than her, with a grown-up family. Apparently they've known one another in a business capacity for some years.'

'I wonder who he is?' Kate murmured, intrigued. 'How typical of Lydia to say nothing, and then just announce out of the blue that she's getting married. I must telephone her now . . .'

'You can't. She'll be in the Seychelles by now. When she rang, she told me they were leaving that afternoon. Oh, how could I have forgotten to tell you. Your father's right,' she added ruefully. 'We are getting old. Oh, Kate, I am sorry . . .'

'It doesn't matter,' Kate reassured her. 'Did she say when she'd be back?'

'Not for at least three weeks.'

Lydia getting married; and after all she'd said about the superiority of the single state! While she was thrilled for her godmother, Kate couldn't help feeling an odd little pang of self-pity. Everyone, it seemed, had someone to love and be loved by, except herself.

But at least she had Cherry, who, instead of going out with her grandfather, had to remain at home with Kate, as he had received an urgent summons from a neighbour who was having problems with his flock.

'Never mind,' Kate consoled her. 'There'll be other market days. Come and help me pick the rest of the raspberries instead.'

'I wonder if Silas has been for Meg yet,' Cherry mused as they worked side by side.

'Probably not yet. I'm not sure how many days he'll have to wait.'

'I hope he'll let me go and see her when she's up

at the farm.' She paused, her forehead creasing. 'I wish we could stay here always, Mum. I don't want to go back to London.' She broke off as they both heard a car coming up the lane.

'Odd . . . I wonder who that can be,' Kate murmured as they heard it turn into the yard and stop.

They sometimes got the odd tourist stopping to ask if they sold fresh food and eggs, and so, opening the door in the wall, Kate walked out of the garden and into the yard with Cherry at her side.

The woman emerging from the driver's seat of the small car was vaguely familiar, but it wasn't until she saw the two gangling teenage boys climbing out of the back that Kate realised why.

Silas's sister and her sons. Her heart started to thump.

'Hello, I'm Susie Oxford. Am I right in thinking that you're Kate Seton?'

'That's right,' Kate agreed. Cherry was standing in front of her and Kate held on to her shoulders, wondering at the grim expression in the other woman's eyes.

'So you must be Cherry. Well, Cherry, I wonder if you could keep my sons entertained for a little while, while I talk with your mother.'

'Well, I suppose I could show them how to train a sheepdog,' Cherry answered airily, darting away from Kate and running over to join the waiting teenagers.

'Shall we?' Susie Oxford invited grimly, taking hold of Kate's arm and almost marching her into the kitchen.

'Look, I've no idea what you want to talk to me about,' Kate protested. What on earth had she done to cause the other woman's obvious antagonism? Unless . . . her body went cold. Unless Silas had for some reason told his sister what had happened the other night, and she disapproved. But by what right? She and Silas were both adults, and neither of them had commitments to anyone else.

'Amazing how different you look from the way I'd imagined. You don't look like a woman who'd throw a man's love in his face and walk off and leave him.'

Kate sat down abruptly, not knowing quite what to make of such an attack.

'Look . . .' she began weakly.

But Susie interrupted her fiercely, saying, 'No . . . *you* look. Or rather, you listen. Eleven years ago, you left my brother flat, breaking off your engagement to him, for heaven knows what reason. You virtually destroyed him then, and now you're doing it again. OK, so then you were only eighteen. I agree that at eighteen everyone is entitled to do something stupid, but I should have thought by now . . .' She broke off. 'Oh, God, can't you *see* how much he loves you, how you're tearing him apart?

'How could you be so callous as to reject Silas because he can't father any children? You already *have* one child. If you're as keen to have this large family as Silas seems to think, aren't you leaving it a bit late to have the others? Don't you care what you're doing to Silas?' she demanded explosively.

Kate simply stared at her, but her face had gone paper-white and her eyes looked haunted. When she tried to stand up, the room swirled violently around her, and she almost fell back into her chair.

'What do you mean, Silas can't father any children?' she whispered huskily.

'You know damn well what I mean. When he was ill in Ethiopia . . .' She broke off, looking appalled as she realised the truth. 'Oh, God, you *didn't* know, did you?'

Kate shook her head, tears stinging her eyes and asked inconsequentially, 'What makes you think he loves me?'

Susie looked at her and gave her a brief smile.

'I don't *think* it. I *know* it. He told me yesterday,' she added quietly, seeing the disbelief warring with hope in Kate's eyes. 'He's never *stopped* loving you, Kate. When you broke your engagement, he said he had to accept your decision, that he couldn't risk seeing you in case he tried to force you to go back to him . . . He finished his PhD, and joined one of the relief organisations and went out to Ethiopia. I think he'd been there about eighteen months when they got in touch with me to tell me he was seriously ill. He'd been wounded by a tribesman's knife. For a while we thought he might die. And then on top of that he contracted a stupid, childish complaint, but there were complications, and he was ill for almost a year. Afterwards . . . well, it meant the end of that kind of fieldwork because of the risk to his health, and his doctors told him that although physically he could make love, he would never be able to father a child.

'At the time, he didn't seem to mind. When I talked to him about it, he said it didn't matter, since he was unlikely to marry. He still loved you, you see,' she told Kate, giving her a direct look.

'I hated you for that,' she told her frankly, and then gave a wry smile. 'When I rang Silas and you answered the phone, you can imagine how I felt. I could hardly believe it! Luckily, we were due up here, anyway. I thought that somehow or other you must have got together and made a fresh start.

'When I asked Silas yesterday how you felt about living so close to your family, and he told me that you wouldn't be moving into the farm with him, I couldn't believe it. When I asked him why, he said it wouldn't be fair to you, that you loved someone else, and that moreover, you wanted more children . . .'

'He told me he was going back to Ethiopia. He told me he didn't want a wife or family,' Kate whispered, stunned.

The two women looked at one another in mute comprehension, and then Kate burst out, 'Of course I'd love children, but surely he could never imagine they'd be more important to me than *him*. Surely he must realise that I love him? What if our positions were reversed?' she demanded fiercely. 'What if I was the one who couldn't conceive? Oh, God, how could he think . . .'

'He told me that you were absolutely devoted to your daughter,' Susie supplied quietly. And then, crossing the distance that separated them, she took hold of Kate's hands. 'I'm so sorry. I had no idea you didn't know. Poor Silas. I suppose he was too proud to tell you. Do you realise that he doesn't even know you love him?'

Because she had told him she loved Cherry's father, Kate realised, her mental wheels turning, as she reviewed everything they had said to one another. So many misunderstandings . . . and the first and most destructive had been her own.

'Did Silas tell you why I broke off our engagement in the first place?' she asked Susie.

The older girl frowned. 'No.'

'I saw him with you and your sons. You were kissing him, and I leapt to the wrong conclusion,' Kate told her wryly.

'And so you left him, without demanding an explanation. But . . .'

'I was eighteen, and insecure, and besides . . .' Kate sighed as she looked out of the window into the stable-yard.

But for Susie's intervention she would have left the Dales without knowing the truth, without knowing why Silas had pretended to her that he was returning to Ethiopia. Without knowing that he loved her.

Her glance strayed to where Cherry was playing with Susie's two sons, gravely instructing them in the correct way to train a potential sheep-dog, and happiness bubbled up inside her like champagne bubbles.

Watching her, Susie saw her expression change and said quietly, 'I should never have interfered.'

Kate turned to her and smiled. 'I'm glad you did. I need to see Silas. Do you know where he is?'

'Up at the farm. He's taking some overdue leave to start making preliminary lists of what's going to need to be done. He thinks we're shopping in the village,' she added wryly. 'Don't go to him out of pity, Kate,' she said seriously. 'He's a man, after all. And I suspect it was your pity he feared when he lied to you. And then there's Cherry,' she added quietly, standing behind Kate to look out at the trio bending over the pup. 'She'll always be a reminder to him that you had a relationship with someone else who was able to give you something he never will.'

All her love and concern for her brother were reflected in her voice and eyes as she spoke, and she was obviously affronted when Kate turned round to face her, a wide smile curling her mouth.

'You will stay here and keep an eye on Cherry for me, won't you?' she said firmly, and there was laughter dancing at the back of her eyes as she added thoughtfully, 'She has several personality traits which I believe are more probably inherited from her father than from me. I *should* be gone long enough for you to recognise most of them.'

Following her gaze, Susie looked out of the window again. Cherry was firmly telling the pup to 'sit' and, heart-stoppingly, as she looked at her, Susie realised exactly what Kate was saying.

'Dear God,' she breathed tearfully. 'She's Silas's.'

But Kate wasn't listening. She was already half-way across the room, car-keys in one hand, her jacket in the other.

Silas had obviously heard her coming. He was standing out in the yard as she drew up, shirt-sleeves rolled up to reveal tanned forearms. There was a smear of dirt across his face and his hair was untidy. He ought to have looked healthily tired, but instead he looked drawn and tense, and her heart ached for him as she got out of the car.

She thought of all the things she had to say to him, and all those she ought to say, and recognised the minefield that such a conversation was likely to be.

Surely what lay between them didn't need finesse—or careful editing?

'I need to talk to you,' she told him quietly. 'Can we go inside?'

Mutely, he led the way. The kitchen was bright with afternoon sunshine. Those units would definitely have to go, she reflected as she followed him past them.

The kitchen opened into a narrow passage which in turn led into an old-fashioned, flagged hallway. The walls and doors were painted shiny cream and looked grimy. That too would have to go, Kate decided energetically as Silas opened the door into the sitting-room, and she caught her breath slightly in pleasure at both the size and the aspect of the room.

It faced south, and still had its original mullioned windows. Beyond them lay what must have once been an entrancing walled garden similar to that at Seton, but slightly smaller. The room's roughly plastered walls glowed pink in the afternoon sun, and even if the parquet floor was uncared for and dull, it didn't take much imagination to see how this room could look with a little thought and a lot of love.

'What was it you wanted to see me about, Kate?' Silas asked her roughly.

There was happiness in her eyes and a spring to her step that made his heart ache with longing.

'Susie's just been to see me,' she told him bluntly. 'I know all about what happened in Ethiopia, Silas. Did you honestly think it would matter a single damn to me?' she demanded fiercely, made brave by her love. 'I love you, Silas.'

She saw him go white and then red, a dark tide of it burning up under his skin, his eyes burning with savage hunger as he looked at her.

He turned his head away and said savagely, 'I don't want your pity, Kate.'

'That's just as well,' she told him drily. 'You aren't being offered it. I need it too much for myself. Have you any *idea* what I've been through these last weeks, knowing that not only had I lost you once, but that I was going to lose you a second time? Over the years I've tried to tell myself that, at eighteen, I wasn't mature enough to know how I felt about you, that time had distorted my views, making my feelings seem more than they had been, but I was wrong.'

She held out her arms to him. For a moment she thought he meant to ignore her, and her heart almost stopped beating. Then he moved and her arms locked round him, her tears flowing freely as she leaned her head on his shoulder.

'Silas . . . Silas . . . How *could* you think I wouldn't love you?'

She looked up at him and saw the pain in his eyes, and her heart started to thump.

'You know that I can't give you a child,' he said sombrely.

Her mouth went dry, her throat felt as though it was packed with cotton wool. Her heart in her mouth, she said huskily, 'You already have . . .'

He stared at her uncomprehendingly, and then said starkly, 'But, Kate, it's impossible. The doctors . . .'

'Cherry is your child,' she told him huskily. 'I was coming to tell you I was pregnant that day when I saw you with Susie. I suppose that because I was already feeling terrified and insecure I immediately leapt to the wrong conclusion . . . and convinced myself that the very last thing you would want to hear from me was that I was carrying your child.'

Silas barely heard her whispered explanation. His fingers gripped her arms as he stared down at her. 'Cherry is mine . . .'

'I'm surprised you didn't realise it. She's like you.'

'And so when you said you still loved her father, you meant me . . .' He said it slowly, with pain and anguish in his voice.

'Yes,' Kate told him simply.

'Oh, dear God,' he groaned. 'Oh, Kate! Kate, what have I done to you?'

'Apart from making me a mother, do you

mean?' she asked him teasingly.

He drew a breath that lifted his chest and expelled it unsteadily.

'Does Cherry know?'

Kate shook her head. 'No,' she told him quietly. 'I didn't think it was fair to tell her when I was convinced that you would soon be gone again. You see, she's already starting to become attached to you, and I didn't want her to suffer the hurt of being rejected.'

For a moment they stood together in silence, and then, from the shelter of his arm, Kate looked out into the garden and said dreamily, 'I think it would be nice to rebuild the wall, don't you? There's something so secret and special about a walled garden, and Cherry will love it. Or am I presuming too much?' she asked directly.

'Never,' Silas told her softly. 'The house and everything in it are yours to do with as you wish.'

'Including you?'

'Including me,' Silas confirmed.

Four days later Silas, Kate and a very excited Cherry went to collect Meg.

'She's going to be my dog and she's going to live at the farm with us,' Kate overheard her telling the receptionist as Silas completed the formalities and Meg was released to them.

Collecting Meg wasn't their only purpose in town. Earlier that day Kate and Silas had been married quietly in the small parish church. Kate's parents, Silas's sister and her family had been the only witnesses, and, although Cherry had accepted the information that Silas was her father with commendable aplomb, Kate worried a little about her lack of reaction.

Now all three of them—four, if one included Meg—were going to live at Silas's house at the institute, until he completed his contract in less than three months' time.

That time would also give them an opportunity to make the farm habitable. Kate's father had been delighted to learn that they would be living so close to them, and had even said gruffly that Silas was 'all right for someone not born in the Dales'. High praise, indeed.

Three days later, when they were all at the farm working, a battered Land Rover drove into the yard, and an angry-looking man got out.

Kate's heart dropped as she saw him, and Meg, who had been in the yard, yelped and skittered away nervously.

Kate recognised the farmer, and so, obviously, did Cherry, who was now holding very firmly on to Meg's collar.

'That's my dog you've got there,' he said without preamble. 'Heard from the postman about how you'd got her. You'd better hand her over or there'll be trouble.'

'The only trouble there's going to be is yours,' Silas said quietly, suddenly appearing round the side of the barn. Kate felt relief flood through her. 'I found that dog wandering on my land some time ago. I had no idea who she belonged to and so I took her to the RSPCA. They got in touch with me last week to say no one had claimed her, and since my daughter has been on at me to get her a dog, I said we'd take it. The dog stays here, Mr Benson,' he added calmly. 'Although the RSPCA did say that they would be very interested in discovering who had owned her, because she'd been rather badly treated.'

Kate saw the man's face change, anger giving way to apprehension.

'Well, mebbe she's not mine at all. Come to think of it, she isn't . . . She'll never make a working dog,' he told them sourly as he climbed into his Land Rover. 'Too timid by half.'

They were all silent as they watched him drive away. Once he had gone, Meg jumped up at Cherry and began licking her hand, and after she had firmly made her sit down Cherry turned to Silas and flung her arms round him, crying, 'Oh, Daddy, you were wonderful! I really thought he was going to take Meg and I was so frightened . . . and so was Mum. Just wait until I tell Gramps!'

Over her head, Kate smiled into Silas's eyes. He bent and ruffled Cherry's hair.

'Happy?' Kate mouthed.

As Cherry detached herself from him and ran across the yard with Meg in tow, he smiled at her.

'More than I can ever say. You've given me a very precious gift, Kate.'

He saw her look at Cherry and smiled.

'Not Cherry, although she is undoubtedly precious. No, the gift I meant was the gift of your love. You've made me whole again. Are you sure you don't mind giving up your job to live here?' he added quietly.

'I like teaching,' she admitted. 'But I'm looking forward to working here with you, Silas . . . building up this farm, doing something that in its way is as worth while as teaching.'

'And you really don't mind the fact that Cherry will always be an only one?'

'Not as long as you don't,' Kate assured him cheerfully. 'At eighteen I was still very much a child, Silas. I looked on the potential children we might have as extensions of ourselves, but children grow up to be people in their own right. I've been lucky with Cherry; I like her as well as love her. I've known children and parents who aren't so lucky. I can honestly say I have no maternal cravings for more children. *You* are the vital essence of my life, Silas. I discovered that a long time ago, and each day that passes only reaffirms it.'

Cherry had disappeared into the barn with Meg. Silas drew Kate into the shadow of the porch.

She melted into his arms, returning his kiss with all the love she felt for him.

'Mum, Dad! Come and watch Meg. I've taught her to beg!'

'Mm . . . I can see what you mean about one being enough,' Silas murmured wryly as Cherry's excited voice warned them that they were about to be interrupted. 'If we had four or more running about I'd never get the chance to kiss you.'

'And that I would object to,' Kate told him.

Arm in arm, they walked across the yard to meet Cherry.

Harlequin Presents

Coming Next Month

Available in September wherever paperback books are sold, or through Harlequin Reader Service:

In the U.S.
901 Fuhrmann Blvd.
P.O. Box 1397
Buffalo, N.Y 14240-1397

In Canada
P.O. Box 603
Fort Erie, Ontario
L2A 5X3

Harlequin American Romance®

The sun, the surf, the sand...

One relaxing month by the sea was all Zoe, Diana and Gracie ever expected from their four-week stay at Gull Cottage, the luxurious East Hampton mansion. They never thought that what they found at the beach would change their lives forever.

Join Zoe, Diana and Gracie for the summer of their lives. Don't miss the GULL COTTAGE trilogy in Harlequin American Romance: #301 CHARMED CIRCLE by Robin Francis (July 1989); #305 MOTHER KNOWS BEST by Barbara Bretton (August 1989); and #309 SAVING GRACE by Anne McAllister (September 1989).

GULL COTTAGE—because one month can be the start of forever...

SWEEPSTAKES RULES & REGULATIONS

NO PURCHASE NECESSARY TO ENTER OR RECEIVE A PRIZE

1. To enter and join the Reader Service, check off the "YES" box on your Sweepstakes Entry Form and return to Harlequin Reader Service. If you do not wish to join the Reader Service but wish to enter the Sweepstakes only, check off the "NO" box on your Sweepstakes Entry Form. Incomplete and/or inaccurate entries are ineligible for that section or sections(s) of prizes. Not responsible for mutilated or unreadable entries or inadvertent printing errors. Mechanically reproduced entries are null and void. Be sure to also qualify for the Bonus Sweepstakes. See rule #3 on how to enter.

2. Either way, your unique Sweepstakes number will be compared against the list of winning numbers generated at random by the computer. In the event that all prizes are not claimed, random drawings will be held from all entries received from all presentations to award all unclaimed prizes. All cash prizes are payable in U.S. funds. This is in addition to any free, surprise or mystery gifts that might be offered. The following prizes are offered: *Grand Prize (1) $1,000,000 Annuity; First Prize (1) $35,000; Second Prize (1) $10,000; Third Prize (3) $5,000; Fourth Prize (10) $1,000; Fifth Prize (25) $500; Sixth Prize (5,000) $5.

   * This Sweepstakes contains a Grand Prize offering of a $1,000,000 annuity. Winner may elect to receive $25,000 a year for 40 years without interest; totalling $1,000,000 or $350,000 in one cash payment. Entrants may cancel Reader Service at any time without cost or obligation to buy.

3. Extra Bonus Prize: This presentation offers two extra bonus prizes valued at $30,000 each to be awarded in a random drawing from all entries received. To qualify, scratch off the silver on your Lucky Keys. If the registration numbers match, you are eligible for the prize offering.

4. Versions of this Sweepstakes with different graphics will be offered in other mailings or at retail outlets by Torstar Corp. and its affiliates. This promotion is being conducted under the supervision of Marden-Kane, Inc., an independent judging organization. By entering this Sweepstakes, each entrant accepts and agrees to be bound by these rules and the decisions of the judges, which shall be final and binding. Odds of winning in the random drawing are dependent upon the total number of entries received. Taxes, if any, are the sole responsibility of the winners. Prizes are nontransferable. All entries must be received by March 31, 1990. The drawing will take place on or about April 30, 1990 at the offices of Marden-Kane, Inc., Lake Success, N.Y.

5. This offer is open to residents of the U.S., United Kingdom and Canada, 18 years or older, except employees of Torstar Corp., its affiliates, subsidiaries, Marden-Kane and all other agencies and persons connected with conducting this Sweepstakes. All Federal, State and local laws apply. Void wherever prohibited or restricted by law.

6. Winners will be notified by mail and may be required to execute an affidavit of eligibility and release, which must be returned within 14 days after notification. Canadian winners will be required to answer a skill-testing question. Winners consent to the use of their name, photograph and/or likeness for advertising and publicity in conjunction with this or similar promotions, without additional compensation.

7 For a list of our most current major prize winners, send a stamped, self-addressed envelope to: Winners List, c/o Marden-Kane, Inc., P.O. Box 701, Sayreville, N.J. 08871.

If Sweepstakes entry form is missing, please print your name and address on a 3" × 5" piece of plain paper and send to:

In the U.S.	In Canada
Sweepstakes Entry	Sweepstakes Entry
901 Fuhrmann Blvd.	P.O. Box 609
P.O. Box 1867	Fort Erie, Ontario
Buffalo, NY 14269-1867	L2A 5X3

LTY-H89
© 1988 Harlequin Enterprises Ltd.